"For heaven's sake, will you stop staring at me?"

"They say appearances are deceptive, and you don't look like a rabid feminist. So tell me, what have you got against men?"

"Not men in general, just some. I particularly dislike the arrogant, presumptuous kind."

He raised an eyebrow. "And is that how you see me?"

ANNABEL MURRAY has pursued many hobbies. She helped found an arts group in Liverpool, England, and appeared in many stage productions before turning her talents to writing an award-winning historical play. She now lives with her husband in Southport, Lancashire, where she enjoys spending time with her two daughters and grandchildren.

Books by Annabel Murray

HARLEQUIN PRESENTS
1148—A PROMISE KEPT
1188—A QUESTION OF LOVE
1228—DON'T ASK WHY
1259—BLACK LION OF SKIAPELOS
1283—ISLAND TURMOIL
1340—LET FATE DECIDE

HARLEQUIN ROMANCE
2717—THE COTSWOLD LION
2782—THE PLUMED SERPENT
2819—WILD FOR TO HOLD
2843—RING OF CLADDAGH
2932—HEART'S TREASURE
2952—COLOUR THE SKY RED

ANNABEL MURRAY

A Man for Christmas

Harlequin Books

TORONTO • NEW YORK • LONDON
AMSTERDAM • PARIS • SYDNEY • HAMBURG
STOCKHOLM • ATHENS • TOKYO • MILAN
MADRID • WARSAW • BUDAPEST • AUCKLAND

A MAN FOR CHRISTMAS
is dedicated to my husband
TOM
my man for 'all seasons'

ISBN 0-373-11613-6

A MAN FOR CHRISTMAS

Copyright © 1992 by Annabel Murray.

CHAPTER ONE

' "On the first day of Christmas my true love sent to me . . ." ' Jodi Knight sang, her voice husky and melodious. As she sang she bounced Tanya, her year-old niece, on her knee. Her reward was the toddler's gummy smile.

Sally, Jodi's elder sister, laughed but protested half seriously, 'You spoil that child! And I haven't got the strength to play rough games with her when you're not around.' She yawned hugely, easing her position in her chair, massaging the small of her back, and groaned. 'I'm sure I never felt this tired when I was expecting Robin—nor when I had Tanya, for that matter.'

'Well, you're years older now, you poor old soul,' Jodi teased lovingly. 'And of course you didn't have two other children to look after when you were expecting Robin.'

'True,' Sally admitted, then sighed, 'and Barry was around more in those days.' Her husband, a civil engineer, was currently working abroad. 'Only three weeks to go until Christmas, and it's unlikely he'll be home in time.'

Jodi looked anxiously at her sister. It wasn't like Sally to make even the smallest complaint about Barry's frequent absences. Some women would have indulged in tears, hysterics, even anger. But Sally, as a rule, had a remarkably placid nature. Obviously the discomforts of pregnancy were having their effect.

'Anyway,' Jodi reverted to their former topic of conversation, 'a bit of fun won't spoil Tanya. So make the most of having me around to take her and Robin off your hands.' She returned to the song and the game.

'Never mind the two turtle doves,' Sally interrupted again. 'What about *your* wants for Christmas? You still haven't given me a list, and I haven't a clue what to get you.'

'Oh, forget presents for me,' Jodi demurred. 'Christmas is for children. Concentrate on them.' And with a smile, 'Don't you think, at twenty-five, I'm a bit too old to be worrying about Father Christmas? Besides, you don't want to be trailing round the shops just now—eight months pregnant and no husband around. When you think about it,' she concluded disgustedly, 'fathers get off jolly lightly. Remember how Dad was always travelling around, and how fed up Mum got?'

Their parents' marriage had ended in a particularly bitter divorce when she and Sally had still been in their teens.

'Dad's travels were to do with his job,' Sally pointed out. 'And Barry would much rather be here if he could. It's not his fault his firm sent him abroad. And you can protest all you like, little sister—you're getting a present. After all, you've no one but family to give them to you. No husband, not even a boyfriend.'

'Thank goodness,' Jodi put in a little grimly. 'Men aren't exactly top of my popularity poll at the moment.'

Sally shook her head despairingly. 'I do wish you wouldn't generalise just because one man let you down. Most men are decent and caring. And as to a present, I owe you,' she continued. 'I don't know what I'd have done without you these last few days.' Sally's doctor had ordered her to rest more if she didn't want to be taken into hospital for the last few weeks of her pregnancy. 'It's really good of you, Jodi,' she continued, 'especially at this time of year, when you must be frantically busy.'

'You don't owe me a thing.' Jodi was indignant. 'We're family, for heaven's sake. You'd do the same for me if—heaven forbid—I was ever in the same predicament.'

'But aren't you a bit worried about leaving Lucinda in charge of the boutique?' asked Sally. 'I mean, she's not turned out to be very reliable as a partner, has she?'

Jodi had first decided she wanted to run her own fashion shop when she was seventeen. Her experience had been gained from working in several of her father's clothing shops up and down the country. Three years ago, together with a friend, she had opened Jodi's Jetset just off Oxford Street, renting a small property belonging to Goodbody's, one of the larger stores.

Jodi pulled a wry face. 'Yes, unfortunately Lucinda's turned out to be a bit of a pain—a rich man's daughter playing at being a businesswoman. She's hardly ever there, and when she is she isn't much help.'

'You don't think she might be losing interest in the whole thing?' Sally suggested.

Jodi nodded. 'Yes, and I just wish I could afford to buy her out, but as I can't... Anyway, she's gone on a skiing holiday over Christmas and New Year, and luckily we have two excellent assistants. I'll pop in to the shop from time to time, but I can trust them to take care of things. So I'm staying right here,' she told her sister, 'for as long as you need me—certainly until you produce my next niece or nephew. Surely Barry could have arranged to be home for that? And it must be ages since he phoned.'

'He can't always get to a phone,' Sally said mildly. 'Some of these sites are hundreds of miles off the beaten track.'

Jodi shook her head wonderingly. 'It's incredible, isn't it, how two sisters as close as we are can have such diametrically opposed views?'

In her teens and early twenties, Sally had enjoyed a flourishing career as a model, in demand and fêted wherever she went. With her youthful face and figure she could have gone on modelling into her thirties. But to Sally her career had been only a stopgap between schooldays and her eventual ambition—marriage and children. Now, five years into that marriage and in the midst of her third pregnancy, Sally looked more 'comfortable' than glamorous.

'How do you mean?' asked Sally.

'Well, it's not that I don't like children. You know I adore Robin and Tanya, but marriage is something I've always relegated to the distant future.' For when she had fulfilled other ambitions—such as travelling around the world—establishing herself in her chosen career.

'I thought you'd changed your mind when you met Rodney,' Sally said regretfully.

About eighteen months previously Rodney Taylor, a successful, attractive man with his own chain of men's clothing stores, had come into Jodi's life, introduced by a mutual friend.

Rodney, pre-warned about Jodi's determination to remain a free spirit, had played his cards carefully, approaching her with a business proposition in the first instance and then as their friendship grew implying that there would not only be a business partnership to look forward to but a lifelong partnership also.

Jodi, once so reluctant to surrender her freedom, had been beguiled by his looks and his glib tongue. She began to dream and plan.

But her plans had been rudely shattered. Just as she was on the verge of admitting and declaring her feelings for him, Rodney's true character had been revealed when suddenly, unexpectedly he was arrested for fraud. Not only was he found to be unscrupulous in his financial dealings, but she had discovered he had actually been living with another girl while still dating her.

Jodi, caught with her defences temporarily down, had been badly hurt, not only in her pride. Her heart too had been bruised. But once she had recovered her equilibrium her defences, particularly her emotional ones, had been doubly reinforced. She had determined never to let any man deceive her again—in business or in a personal relationship.

Sally had experienced no such traumas, but even so her life wasn't easy.

'I don't know how you put up with everything,' Jodi exclaimed suddenly. 'Three pregnancies in four years, Barry away so much—how can you be so calm—so accepting?'

Sally smiled indulgently. 'Because I love children and I love Barry. If you love someone you'll put up with quite a lot. Maybe you'll find that out one day.

And I know Barry will phone the moment he gets an opportunity.' She looked searchingly at her sister. 'I'd love to see you as happy as I am, Jodi. I do wish you'd fall in love with someone.'

'I did once, remember?' Jodi's tone was bitter. 'Or thought I had. I had a lucky escape there. Apart from anything else, I could have lost my business.'

'Yes, it's a great pity that happened. But not all men are alike. And besides, I'm not talking about a business partnership—the two things don't necessarily have to be combined. I'm talking about love. You don't know what you're missing. Maybe,' Sally said jokingly, 'you should put something like that top of your "wants" list when you write to Santa—a man.'

'A man? For Christmas?' Jodi snorted derisively. 'No, thank you. I've never been in any rush to be tied down, and after Roddy... But you old married women are just the same—can't wait to see everyone else in the same boat.'

'Less of the "old", if you please. I'm only two years older than you. Anyway, it won't be easy to pair you off. Any man you married would have to be different from the usual run of men. He'd have to be very tolerant, especially if you insist on continuing your career after marriage. And he'll need to be strong too—to match your tough streak.'

'Tough?' Jodi exclaimed humorously. It was the last way she would have described herself, but then not even to Sally had she ever revealed the depths of her vulnerability—a vulnerability she now sought to hide beneath a defensive shell. 'You make me sound like something off a butcher's slab—or one of these square-shouldered soap-opera heroines.'

Sally chuckled. 'One might be forgiven for agreeing with the last bit—the career-woman image you project. I've always felt sorry for the strings of men who pant after you. But I didn't say you were tough through and through. You've got your soft side too, or you wouldn't be here now. And you're good with kids. You ought to have some of your own before you're too——'

'Talking of children...' Jodi stood up, anxious to avoid a lecture she was only too familiar with, 'I promised to take Robin into town. I noticed that Griffiths Brothers, just round the corner from us, are starting their Christmas Grotto today. Robin's got quite a list for Santa. Should I take Tanya too?'

Sally shook her head. 'She's too young to appreciate it this year, and you'll have your hands quite full enough with Robin. He can be a little demon at times.'

'Is my daddy coming back soon?' her nephew wanted to know as she buttoned him into his raincoat.

Jodi bit her lip, uncertain how to reply. She wanted to reassure the anxious small boy, banish that worried look from his eyes. The concept of time was so hard for young children to understand. But if she told him 'yes' and Barry didn't materialise for several more weeks... Such a pity Sally—like their mother—had married a man whose work took him away so much.

On the other hand, to be absolutely fair to her brother-in-law, that work had provided Sally with this lovely home—and property wasn't cheap in Hampstead. Jodi often wished she could afford to live in this delightful old village with its tortuous streets and its picturesque houses which mixed the grand and the spacious with cottages—some of them covetably pretty.

'Will he, Auntie Jodi?' Robin persisted.

'I hope so,' seemed to be a safe answer.

It was a wet murky Saturday afternoon, more like January than December. But the large stores along busy Oxford Street were brightly lit and the street itself was glittering with illuminations. Garish pink clowns on tightropes juggling flashing balls vied for attention with rotund Santas and red-nosed reindeer. To attempt to hurry through the turgidly moving crowds drifting in and out of chromium, neon and glass façades was to court frustration.

On the train in from Hampstead, four-year-old Robin, his worries forgotten, had behaved angelically. But now, as they neared their destination, he was getting more and more excited, dragging at Jodi's hand.

Jodi would have liked to pop round the corner to reassure herself that all was well at the boutique, but her nephew was getting impatient. 'Is this the shop?' he asked every few yards.

At last, 'Here we are,' she said thankfully.

The warmth and colour of the store reached out to envelop them as they pushed through the heavy doors. With an indulgent smile, Jodi watched her small nephew's face as he gazed about him at the lights of many hues reflected in the tinsel festooning the counters. The air seemed perfumed with a thousand smells, a unique mixture of everything that was on sale.

Santa's Grotto, Jodi discovered, was in the toy department on the sixth floor, reached by a lift crammed with other small, damp, excited children escorted by resigned adults with unpleasantly dripping umbrellas.

Around the grotto bedlam reigned. Despite her affection for her nephew, Jodi was unused to children in large numbers, and she winced at the sheer volume of noise. Her admiration went out to the devoted helpers, elderly women dressed a little incongruously as elves, whose job it was to shepherd youngsters of all ages past the upholstered throne where the store's Father Christmas sat in state, surrounded by colourfully wrapped parcels.

He was a very splendid Father Christmas. No tacky old costume here, looking as if it had been worn by centuries of Santas. In fact, it looked as if no expense had been spared to make this one of the most attractive grottoes she had ever seen.

But as she and Robin joined the queue it suddenly struck Jodi that the hubbub was not a happy one. Several small children who had already visited Santa were crying piteously; some were screaming with temper. A curly-haired little girl who looked as though ordinarily butter wouldn't melt in her mouth was in mid-tantrum, lying on the floor and drumming her heels. Mothers and grandparents were gathered in angry conclave, watched curiously by those whose children had not yet reached the throne.

Meanwhile Father Christmas could be seen agitatedly mopping his brow and one of the 'elves' was wringing despairing hands while the others stood helplessly by.

'There seems to be some problem,' Jodi suggested to the elderly woman in front of her.

'Problem!' the woman grumbled. 'More like total disaster. D'you know, we've been waiting in this queue for half an hour now and they still haven't sorted it out. If it wasn't for her,' she indicated the small girl whose hand she held, 'I'd give it up as a bad job and go home.'

'What's wrong exactly?'

'A mix-up in the parcels. Boys are getting things like dolls and hairslides in their parcels and the girls are getting train sets or footballs. Someone must have wrapped them in the wrong coloured paper.'

'And what's been done about it?'

'Not a lot. The staff seem to be in a complete panic. They're only part-timers, of course, pensioners taken on just for the season.'

'It's probably not their fault, then,' Jodi said. 'Management should be sorting it out.'

The woman nodded. 'That's what I thought. But no one wants to lose their place in the queue to go and tell them.'

'Well, somebody's got to do something,' Jodi decided. And since no one else seemed inclined to take positive steps it had better be her.

She was always swift to sum up situations and decide on a course of action. Carrying Robin in her arms, she strode towards the dais. She set the child down by the plush throne, then picked up a toy trumpet discarded by some disappointed child. Infant lungs might not have achieved such spectacular effect, but Jodi managed to produce a long loud blast.

There was a surprised silence into which Jodi announced, 'If you'll all keep calm for a minute, I'll get the management to sort this out.'

Unfortunately this announcement did not have the desired effect. At once the adults surged towards her,

each one bent on making his or her grievances known
to this self-appointed advocate.

To make things worse, Father Christmas and his
attendants, misunderstanding the purpose of the mass
advance, cravenly slipped away, leaving Jodi in sole
possession of the dais—and an enterprising Robin in
possession of the throne.

In vain Jodi raised her hands pleading for silence,
but no one would cede the floor to his or her
neighbour.

'*Quiet*!' The stentorian bellow achieved the impossible, and as one the churning mob turned to seek
the source of this impressive noise.

A man stood in the entrance of the toy department,
and having secured their attention he advanced
through the crowd, head and shoulders above most
of them.

No pocket Venus herself, Jodi decided that he was
certainly taller than average—a real hunk of a man.
But it was not just his height which compelled her
gaze. He wasn't classically handsome—both mouth
and nose were a shade too large for that—nevertheless there was something compelling about him
that, Jodi guessed, would draw women to him in
droves. Dark auburn hair flopped over a high intel-
ligent forehead and he wore a silvery grey suit of impeccable cut. One of the floorwalkers?

As he crossed the department his undoubtedly angry
gaze never left Jodi. She was very visible in her el-
evated position on the dais, and striking-looking in
her turquoise winter coat, her straight silky blonde
hair spilling over the collar.

As he mounted the dais something absolute about
his air of authority kept the hitherto vocal customers

silent. But at first he did not address them. Instead he turned on Jodi, his words for her only, his tone condemnatory.

'What the hell do you mean by inciting this uproar? What kind of a rabble-rouser are you?'

Jodi gasped indignantly. 'I didn't start this,' she began. 'My nephew and I——'

'Oh, no?' He chose to be sarcastic. 'That, of course, is why you're standing up here conducting the proceedings.'

'For your information,' Jodi said icily, 'I was trying to help. I——'

'Help? In that case I'd hate to see you in an *un-helpful* mood!' With that he turned his back on her and addressed the still strangely quiet customers. 'Now, ladies and gentlemen—my name is Griffiths, David Griffiths. Would one of you—one,' he emphasised, 'kindly tell me what all this is about.'

To Jodi's chagrin, whereas all her efforts had achieved nothing, his words had the desired effect, and an elderly man appointed himself spokesperson, receiving a courteous hearing. The elderly man's words vindicated her behaviour. Yet by not so much as a flicker of his gaze did this David Griffiths acknowledge the fact. Jodi seethed.

'Thank you. That's all quite clear now. As I told you, my name is Griffiths and I'm the managing director here. So I can assure you that this problem will be speedily dealt with.'

He sprang lithely down from the dais and spoke rapidly into an inter-departmental telephone. It was impossible to hear what he was saying, and Jodi didn't really care. She was too angry. With Robin she had rejoined the cluster of customers. If it hadn't been for disappointing her nephew she would have left Griffiths Brothers' store immediately. How dared David Griffiths blame her for his store's inefficiency?

'Right, ladies and gentlemen,' he had all their attention once more, 'the staff dining-room has been placed at your disposal. If you would all adjourn there—for ten minutes at the most—refreshments will be served, on the house. By that time the grotto will have a fresh supply of correctly wrapped, suitable presents for your children.' His tone implied that, if such were not the case, heads would roll. 'My assistant,' he indicated a glamorous young woman who had appeared within seconds of his telephone call, 'will show you the way.'

As the now orderly crowd fell in behind the young woman, Jodi found that she and Robin were being prevented from joining them.

'Not you,' David Griffiths said. 'I'd like you and your nephew to accompany me to my office.' His hand at her elbow was impersonal yet firm. But Jodi found his touch oddly disconcerting. She resisted.

'Why?' she demanded. If he was still seeing her as a troublemaker...

To her surprise he smiled ruefully, and for the first time—now that they were not darkened by anger—she noticed that his eyes were of the most amazing shade of green, crystal-clear and fringed by thick dark lashes that a woman might have envied.

'Because I seem to owe you an apology.'

Jodi still stood her ground. 'You do,' she agreed, 'but I don't want any preferential treatment. I'll join the others.'

'No, please,' his grasp tightened, 'you must allow me to make amends.' He smiled, and the smile altered his face, banishing the grimness, making him even more attractive than she had at first supposed. 'Otherwise how will I know I'm forgiven?'

Jodi was not one to bear a grudge—except perhaps in Rodney's case. Now her earlier anger had evaporated, and this man really did seem genuinely apologetic. She shrugged, 'Oh, very well,' and allowed herself to be steered towards the lift.

His office was very much like the man, large and very masculine. David Griffiths motioned Jodi and Robin towards a large leather chesterfield, then, ignoring the massive executive desk, he seated himself in a matching leather armchair. No sooner were they seated than tea was brought in.

'Orange juice for the little boy?' David Griffiths asked. 'I believe you did say he's your nephew?'

Jodi nodded. 'There's really no need for all this,' she said. 'I——'

He held up one hand. 'But I think there is. In the heat of the moment I did you an injustice. But you must admit,' he smiled as he passed her cup, inviting her to share the joke, 'to anyone coming suddenly upon the scene, hearing all that noise, seeing your lofty position, it did look——'

'As though I was...what was the term you used? Oh yes, a "rabble-rouser".' Jodi said it feelingly. She might forgive, but it was an insult she was not likely to forget in a hurry.

'Was that what I said? Again, I can only apologise. As I said, in the heat of the moment...' He shrugged, then reached into the inside pocket of his impeccably cut jacket and pulled out a notebook. 'And now,' briskly, 'to business. Your name and address, please.'

Jodi stared at him, 'What on earth do you want that for?'

'Standard procedure. All those customers inconvenienced by this afternoon's incident will receive an official letter of apology.'

'There's no need for you to write to me,' she told him. 'You've already apologised.'

'I've given you my personal verbal apology, yes, but we at Griffiths Brothers believe in doing things properly. So, your name?' He waited, lifting an eyebrow.

'Jodi. Jodi Knight. And this is Robin.'

'Jodi,' he repeated as he wrote it down. He seemed to linger over it, and she rather liked the way he said it, his deep voice appreciative as though he found the name to his taste. 'An unusual name. But then I suspect you're an unusual woman?' His eyes quizzed her.

Jodi stiffened. She was familiar with that kind of approach, one she always firmly crushed. 'I don't think so,' she said coolly.

Since she was acting in *loco parentis*, she gave him Sally's address. She knew that large stores sometimes accompanied their apologies to customers by goods or vouchers, and Sally might as well have the benefit of them. And besides, living alone as she did, Jodi rarely volunteered the address of her own flat.

'And now,' he glanced at his wristwatch, 'I think order should have been restored in the toy department. Shall we?'

He took no chances, remaining on the dais to the side of the throne, very obviously on a watching brief as the long queue reformed around the grotto.

Robin's turn came. He climbed on to Santa's prof-
fered knee and in a stage whisper listed most of the
items Jodi had expected. But, as a fond and responsible aunt, she kept a careful mental note of a few
things she and her sister had overlooked. It wrenched
her heart when to his wants he added, 'And I want
my daddy to come back.'

'And what would his auntie like for Christmas?' a
deep voice enquired suddenly.

Startled, Jodi realised that David Griffiths had
moved to the front edge of the dais and was talking
to her. His unusual green eyes had undergone yet
another change—they were openly amused at her af-
fronted reaction.

But instead of giving him the set-down another man
might have received, she decided to ignore his
question. Instead she held out a hand to Robin. 'Come
on, darling, you've had your turn. There are other
boys and girls waiting.'

But instead of encountering Robin's tiny paw she
found her fingers taken in the warm clasp of a strong
shapely hand. A strange sensation zipped through her,
as her heart set up the most unexpected thudding, and
she tried to retrieve her hand, the left one, and found
her efforts resisted. David Griffiths' thumb was in-
specting with deceptive casualness the ringless state
of her third finger.

She knew, from previous experience, exactly what
that portended. Next he would be asking for a date.
At the thought she was overtaken by a sudden feeling
of breathlessness.

'Let go!' she whispered fiercely, and looked uncomfortably around her. 'People are watching.

Children are watching,' she added, hoping this would restore him to a sense of decorum.

Then to her relief Robin, clutching a large parcel, rejoined her, her hand was released and she hurried away, embarrassed and angry again, aware of the odd glances she was receiving from other customers. What must they think of the preferential treatment she had received—first being taken into his private office and then this . . . ? Her hand still seemed to tingle from the contact with warm male fingers.

She was annoyed, but by the time the lift reached the ground floor she had regained her poise and her normal off-beat sense of humour had reasserted itself.

After all, as she told her sister later, 'It can't be many people who've had a pass made at them in Santa's Grotto!'

She might joke about it. But it was strange how the incident—one she would normally have dismissed—stayed with her all that evening. All too frequently she found her thoughts invaded by the recollection of a pair of startling green eyes. Almost she could still feel the touch of that strong warm hand, hear the sound of a deep voice.

Finally, irritated with herself for such uncharacteristic behaviour, she made a determined effort to banish the memory, deliberately channelling that irritation towards David Griffiths. He'd had no business taking advantage of the situation. It was sheer sexual harassment. And if she had been one of his own employees she would have complained about it.

The letter of apology came on Monday, formal, impeccably polite, obviously stereotyped, nothing in it to which anyone could take exception. And that was all. No personal touch. The letter had probably been sent out to all the complainants by his secretary. Jodi was obscurely disappointed.

'Well, that's that,' she said, handing the official notepaper to her sister. 'The end of an episode—and,' she made a joke of it, 'no freebies.'

Sally looked at her curiously, but made no comment.

On Tuesday morning the flowers came, a ridiculously large bouquet of them, their warm exotic scent filling the room.

'Red roses!' Sally was awed. 'At this time of year. They must have cost a fortune. Who on earth's your secret admirer? What does it say?' she asked eagerly as Jodi retrieved the deckle-edged card which had slipped down among the stems.

' "Just to reinforce my apology—and in the hope that we may become better acquainted." Oh!' As her heart skipped a beat Jodi crushed the card in her hand.

'David Griffiths?' Sally asked.

'Yes,' she replied as evenly as her shaken senses would allow. It was gratifying to think that he still remembered their encounter, but Jodi could have done without this reminder of a man who had already done much to disrupt her serenity.

'I think it's very romantic,' Sally said. 'You must have made a very strong impression on him.'

'Oh, I did,' Jodi said drily. 'He called me a rabble-rouser, remember?' She essayed humour to cover up just how much the flowers and the message had shaken her normal poise. 'As for romantic...'

Sally eyed her curiously. 'Do you intend to go on warding off men's advances for ever?'

'This sort of advance, certainly—from someone I don't know. And I know nothing about David Griffiths. A man of his age—mid-thirties, I'd say— could be engaged, married even.'

'Which is making you more cross?' Sally asked shrewdly. 'His attentions, or the fact that you don't know if he's free to pay them?'

Jodi preferred not to examine that question. 'I just don't like presumption from men I don't know.'

Sally wasn't satisfied with that excuse. 'All the men you do know you treat the same way as you treat your women friends.'

'Much the best way,' Jodi said briskly. 'Good friends, no romantic nonsense—just mutual respect and consideration. We're all individuals, not looking to be paired off.'

'Well,' said Sally, 'I have a feeling you'll be getting to know David Griffiths much better before long.' She indicated the flowers. 'I bet he'll be following those up in person before long.'

Inexplicably, Jodi shivered. But, 'He'd better not,' she retorted. 'We don't want him turning up on your doorstep.'

'I wouldn't mind in the least,' Sally said. 'Come on, Jodi, just because one man turned out to be a rotter... Oh, that Rodney has a lot to answer for! But don't let that incident ruin your whole life, make you afraid of falling in love again.'

'I'm not afraid,' Jodi denied, much too strenuously. 'It's just that I don't want to be caged, possessed. Remember how possessive Mum was with

Dad? I don't want to lose my privacy, the control of my own life. I'm quite happy as I am, thank you.'

But there was more than a grain of truth in what Sally said, she admitted to herself later. She didn't want her emotional equanimity disrupted again by all the things that seemed to accompany a love affair—insecurity, jealousy, heartache, betrayal. Apart from her parents' turbulent marriage, her own unhappy experience with Rodney, she'd seen so many of her friends suffer that way.

That afternoon Sally received a telephone call. When she returned to the living-room, Jodi looked up enquiringly, then sprang to her feet.

'What is it? You look awful. Hey, it's not the baby, is it? You're not starting early?'

'No such luck.' Sally's lower lip trembled, but with a warning nod towards Robin, busy with his toys, she controlled herself. 'Th-that was Barry. The contract's not running to schedule. Oh, Jodi,' Sally's eyes, the same shade of grey as her sister's, were swimming with tears, 'he might not be back until well into the New Year. I'm sorry,' she hiccuped, 'to be so stupid. Normally I can cope. But I did hope he'd be back in time for...' Wordlessly now she indicated her distended abdomen.

Jodi put an arm around her sister. 'Look, why don't I ring Barry back and——?'

'No.' Miserably Sally shook his head. 'It wouldn't do any good. If he says he can't come, then he can't.'

As she bathed Robin that night and heard his bedtime prayers—which included his usual plea for his daddy to come back—Jodi thanked her stars she was not so

totally dependent on someone else for her happiness
and peace of mind. She knew how Sally, despite all
her determined efforts not to show it, worried about
her husband when he was abroad.

The doorbell rang just as she was coming out of
Robin's bedroom.

'I'll get it!' she called to Sally, whom she'd persuaded to put her feet up.

It was dark in the porch. Damn, she'd meant to
replace the lamp. 'Yes?' she said enquiringly to the
dark silhouette on the doorstep.

'Hello, Jodi,' was the totally unexpected answer.
Just the two words, but the deep voice rang a warning
chord, and as he moved into the light from the hallway
she saw him. David Griffiths. All at once she was very
much aware of him and the way he towered over her.

With a purely instinctive reaction of self-protection
she made to shut the door in his face. But a large foot
and a strong hand prevented her from doing so.

'I'd hoped,' he said drily, 'for a warmer welcome
than that.'

Jodi gave up the unequal struggle with the door.
She was no weakling, but he was far stronger. She
was slightly breathless as she said, 'I don't know what
you're doing here, and I wish you wouldn't——'

'Jodi, who is it?'

She turned. Sally had come out into the hall, her
expression contorted with anxiety.

'You're . . . you're not a policeman, are you?' she
demanded. 'Nothing's happened to . . . to . . .'

'No,' Jodi reassured her quickly. 'No, he's not a
policeman.' She vacated her defensive position in the
doorway and moved to her sister's side, putting a re-

assuring hand on her shoulder. 'This,' she said, 'is Mr Griffiths.'

'Oh!' Sally moved forward, regarding him with frank interest. 'So you're the one who sent Jodi the flowers?'

'Guilty,' he agreed.

Sally subjected him to a close appraisal. 'Yes, I think I would have recognised you from her description. I've been dying to meet you.'

Jodi felt uncomfortable. Now David Griffiths would get the impression that she had been sufficiently interested in him to give her sister an itemised account of his appearance. She wished Sally would go and sit down again and leave her to deal with this intrusion.

'Do come in, Mr Griffiths,' Sally invited, somewhat unnecessarily.

For he had taken advantage of Jodi's concern for her sister to make good his position. Now, with the front door closed behind him, he seemed to be occupying a large part of the hallway, his head brushing the overhead garlands. The Christmas decorations were up a little early, in Jodi's opinion, but Sally had decreed that they go up for Robin's sake.

David Griffiths, Jodi noticed inconsequentially, was standing just beneath the bunch of mistletoe she'd hung only that evening.

He was too quick. He followed her gaze, saw the object of it and smiled, but to her relief he made no comment, going up a notch in her estimation. A lot of men would have made some fatuous remark.

'Most people—my friends, that is—call me Griff,' he told Sally as he followed her into the living-room. He looked around him appreciatively. 'Nice house. I like Hampstead. A friend of mine has a house actually in the village.'

'We were just about to eat,' Sally told him. 'Would you like to join us?'

Jodi knew her face must be betraying her consternation. What did Sally think she was up to, encouraging this man?

To her relief he declined the invitation. 'Thanks, but I've already eaten. Sorry if I've called at an inconvenient moment.' And to Jodi, 'I just wanted to make sure my roses had arrived safely. But I see they have.'

'Yes—thank you. You shouldn't have bothered,' she said gruffly, aware of sounding stiff and ungrateful.

He considered her reflectively. 'It doesn't sound as if they achieved the desired effect.' And as she made no reply, 'Wouldn't you like to know why I sent them?'

'No,' she said quickly. She was afraid he might be about to tell her anyway. Her heart had begun to beat most erratically. Cravenly, she edged towards the door. 'That is...I assumed they were part of the store's "official apology". Er—wasn't that Robin I heard?' she muttered hopefully, but received no support from her sister.

'No. Once he's asleep he never wakes—neither of them does. Look, Griff, since you've already eaten, would you like to come round tomorrow evening instead?' asked Sally.

Jodi could cheerfully have throttled her sister. But again David Griffiths was shaking his head.

'Much as I'd like to, I have a previous engagement. Maybe I could take a rain-check?' At last he was moving back into the hallway. Jodi could hardly wait for him to be gone so she could take Sally to task.

On the threshold he turned. 'Next time I see you,' he told Jodi, 'I'll explain something to you.' And, as she looked at him uncomprehendingly, 'I'll tell you exactly why I sent you the roses.' And before she could gasp out a disclaimer, tell him he wouldn't be seeing her again, he was gone.

CHAPTER TWO

THE moment the door closed behind David Griffiths, Jodi turned reproachfully to her sister.

'What on earth possessed you?' she demanded. 'Inviting him in—*and* inviting him for a meal.'

'I liked him,' Sally said simply. 'He's just the kind of——'

'Well, *you* can have him. I——'

'Thanks, but *I* just want Barry.' Suddenly Sally looked very tired and depressed, and at once Jodi was contrite.

'Oh, I'm sorry, love. I'm a tactless, bad-tempered bitch.'

Sally patted her sister's arm. 'No, you're not—not usually. But Griff has really got to you, hasn't he?' She looked curiously at Jodi. 'And I can't help asking myself why. It's not like you to lose your cool—and especially not where a man's concerned. Could it be,' she speculated, 'that you're attracted to him but don't want to admit it?'

'Certainly not.' Not even to herself would Jodi admit anything so disturbing. 'I just don't like pushy people.' She was aware that, as an excuse, it was a pretty feeble one.

'He's certainly not backward in coming forward,' Sally agreed. 'But maybe that's the sort you need, to break down those barriers of yours.'

Jodi was having difficulty in not losing her temper—and with her sister, of all people. Besides being her

sister, Sally was also her best friend. And it was all
that man's fault.

'For heaven's sake let's forget about him,' she said.

Easier said than done. For the rest of that evening,
insidiously, thoughts of David Griffiths returned to
plague her. Something about him made her feel dis-
turbingly vulnerable and a little afraid. Afraid of
what? Immediately she knew the answer—afraid of
being hurt again.

It was not, Jodi told herself in the days that followed,
that she expected or even wanted to hear from Griff—
David Griffiths, she corrected herself. Griff was what
his friends called him. She didn't qualify for that title.
No, she wasn't expecting to hear, but when two or
three days had passed without any communication she
was aware of an unreasonable pique, which, however,
did not stop her scrutiny of the mail delivery each
morning.

On Friday the letterbox gave its familiar rattle and
thud. Surreptitiously, Jodi glanced at Sally. Busy
feeding Tanya and admonishing Robin to get on with
his own food, her sister seemed to be unaware that
the postman had called.

'I'm not sure,' Jodi said casually, 'but I thought I
heard the post. Do you want me to look?'

The mail was a heavy one. Jodi sifted quickly
through it. Square white envelopes in the main.
Christmas cards addressed to her sister and brother-
in-law—cards Barry probably wouldn't be home in
time to see. She hoped the thought would not occur
to Sally and upset her. There was also an envelope
bearing only her sister's name—addressed in a familiar hand.

For a moment Jodi was tempted to hide it. But deceit was foreign to her nature. And—she had to admit—she was a little put out, and curious too as to why David Griffiths should be writing to her sister. Slowly she returned to the breakfast-room.

Soon Sally was busy ripping envelopes. The one addressed to her alone she had put to one side. Time and again Jodi's eyes were drawn to it with unwilling fascination. But at last Sally picked it up and in doing so glanced across at her sister, surprising Jodi's intent expression. She looked from her sister back to the letter in her hand.

'What's wrong? You're looking at me as if this was a letter bomb.' Then, a smile spreading slowly across her face, 'Oh-oh! You wouldn't happen to know who it's from?'

Jodi was annoyed to find herself colouring. 'Well, I——'

'Is it from Griff, by any chance?' And as Jodi nodded, 'Would you like to open it?'

'Certainly not.'

The envelope and the notepaper it contained were of good quality, Jodi noticed, but she feigned lack of interest as her sister studied the contents. Sally chuckled, then pushed the letter across the table. Curiosity warring with reluctance, this time Jodi accepted it. The message was a brief one.

'I'm free to dine with you one evening this weekend.' A signature and a telephone number were written underneath.

'Cheek!' muttered Jodi, but her heart had skipped a beat and she was aware that anticipation was mingled with her indignation.

'Well?' Sally demanded.

'Well what?'

'Shall I invite him?'

Feigning total indifference, Jodi shrugged. 'Do as you like. It's your house.'

Sally made an exasperated gesture. 'And it's your life. You know, I have a feeling that, once he's in it, you won't get him out so easily.'

Jodi snorted derisively. 'That's what you think, Sis. Nobody bulldozes Jodi Knight into anything. Ask him to dinner if you want to, but it won't get him any-where. Come on, little 'un,' she said to Robin, 'time I took you to playgroup.'

'I've fixed it,' Sally said later as the sisters sipped their mid-morning coffee. 'Tomorrow evening.'

This time Jodi did not pretend not to know what she meant. 'I've been thinking—you shouldn't be making extra work for yourself right now.' She was sincere in that, but if she'd hoped to change her sister's mind she failed.

'I'm not making work for me,' Sally said calmly. 'You can cook the dinner—your chance to show off your skills!'

Jodi raised her eyebrows. 'Oh, thanks very much,' she said drily, 'but I've no particular desire to show off in front of David Griffiths. And aren't you taking a bit of a risk? How do you know I won't spike his food? That'd put him off for good.'

Sally laughed. 'I'll chance it. I don't see you as the female poisoner of the century, somehow. Anyway, I think you protest too much. Go on, admit it, he in-trigues you.'

'Well,' Jodi said, 'I am curious to see just how far he's prepared to go to ingratiate himself. But that's all,' she added hastily.

'What are we having?' Sally peered curiously into the heavily laden shopping basket.

'You can just wait until this evening,' Jodi told her, whisking the basket away, 'as penance for aiding and abetting the man.'

Jodi enjoyed cooking. In her own home she entertained regularly, male and female friends alike, and cooking for one man, therefore, should have presented no difficulties. So why had she agonised for so long over her shopping list? So why, Sally demanded, was it so important that every dish be prepared to an unheard-of peak of perfection?

'You've been in that kitchen for simply hours. Hadn't you better think about getting yourself ready? It's you he's coming to see, after all.'

'No rush. Besides, he can take me as he finds me. I don't want him thinking I'm anxious to impress.' Jodi glanced casually at the kitchen clock, then did a double-take. She had precisely half an hour before David Griffiths arrived.

She might deny the necessity of looking her best before him. But on the other hand she didn't want to appear in the scruffy jeans and sweater to which evidences of her cooking now clung. A glance in the hall mirror as she hurried towards the stairs told her also that she had flour on her flushed face and that her normally sleek hair was decidedly dishevelled.

Usually Jodi looked forward to entertaining. She was of a naturally sociable disposition. But she was not looking forward to this evening, and it was all that man's fault. He made her uncomfortable, uncharacteristically uncertain of herself.

Even so, she couldn't help wondering about him. Was he unattached, free to pursue her? Just what did he have in mind? And why her? Oh, bother it, she hadn't time to speculate on what made David Griffiths tick.

To look at her now, she told herself with satisfaction twenty minutes later, no one would guess she had spent several hours labouring over a hot stove. Wearing her favourite dress—simple but sophisticated in black—her gleaming blonde hair braided and swept up around her head, she felt totally composed and in charge of herself.

The doorbell rang as she descended the stairs, producing, to her annoyance, a faint fluttering sensation in her stomach.

'Be a love and get that,' Sally called from Tanya's bedroom. 'She's being a little demon tonight—won't settle.'

Jodi drew in a deep steadying breath, then moved to comply. The open doorway was filled by an enormous cellophane-wrapped bouquet. Behind it David Griffiths was just visible.

'I wish you wouldn't do this,' Jodi said uncomfortably. 'I don't think you should be spending money on me. I——'

'I haven't,' he said disconcertingly. 'These are for my hostess—your sister.'

'Oh.' Feeling unutterably foolish, she stood aside and let him enter. 'Sally will be down in a moment.' She turned on her heel and stalked into the lounge. Every step of the way she was uncomfortably aware of him following close behind. All the poise upon which she had been congratulating herself vanished as she imagined his eyes surveying her retreating back view. She sat down on the settee, then wished she hadn't. He might construe her choice of seat as an invitation to join her.

He set the flowers down on a side-table. And now he was not obscured by them she was able to observe him. Another impeccably cut suit—dark this time—somehow emphasising the sheer size of him—large and very, very masculine.

'The flowers weren't for you,' he said again, moving towards her. 'But this is.' He held out a small exquisitely wrapped package.

Jodi shook her head. 'Oh, no...I can't. It's not right—I hardly know you.'

'It doesn't carry any strings,' he told her. 'Call it an early Christmas present if you like.'

'There's no earthly reason for you to be giving me Christmas presents now—or then,' she told him. 'Presents are for family, close friends——'

'By the time Christmas comes, I hope we will be close friends,' he said calmly.

'We won't. I——'

'Oh, come now. If I really believed that I should be greatly disappointed.' He smiled, one of those charming smiles of his, and Jodi was glad she had chosen to sit. His smiles were decidedly knee-weakening. 'I hate disappointments,' he went on lightly, 'ever since I was a small boy and I didn't get the shiny red tractor I'd asked for. Here!' As she'd feared, he sat down beside her and pressed the package into her palm, closing her fingers over it. 'I'm not taking it back,' he said. 'I wouldn't like having to admit that my girlfriend had refused it.'

'I'm not your——'

'But you're going to be,' he said with cool assurance.

Jodi stared at him in frustration. How did you argue with someone like this, someone who absolutely refused to be dissuaded? Abruptly she stood up and set the parcel down on the table beside the flowers.

'Aren't you going to open it?' he asked.

'I . . . maybe . . . later.'

'Sorry, but that's not good enough. When I give people presents I like to see them open them.' He rose too, picked up the discarded package and tore off the wrappings to reveal a small jeweller's box. He flipped up the lid and held it out, so close that she could not avoid looking at its contents.

On a nest of cotton wool lay a dainty marcasite brooch. It was very beautiful, but the design . . . ?

'Mistletoe,' he said, as if that explained everything. 'It will have to do until I can persuade you to join me underneath the real thing. Here, let me put it on for you.' With deft fingers for such large hands he pinned the brooch to the shoulder of her dress, and a sensation that was purely erotic zipped through her as, unavoidably, she felt the warmth of his hands through the thin material.

Dismayed at her own involuntary response, she stepped back. And stepped back too quickly, catching her heel on the edge of a rug. She would have fallen but for his quick reactions. With his hands firmly holding her upper arms she was far too close to him for comfort, and he seemed to be in no hurry to let go of her, those startling green eyes of his compelling her gaze.

Jodi swallowed nervously. Despite the irregularity of his features, somehow he still managed to exude this lethal attraction. The scent of him came to her nostrils, compounded of warm male, of expensive masculine cologne. There was sensuality in those eyes, in the full lower lip of that mobile mouth.

As though he sensed her discomfort at his proximity he smiled widely, revealing even white teeth, and the grasp of his hands tightened, seemed to bring her closer.

'Don't mind me,' Sally said cheerfully, halting on the threshold of the room as she took in the deceptively intimate little scene.

With an exclamation of dismay, Jodi wrenched herself free, angry colour running up under her normally pale skin. 'Pour Mr Griffiths a drink, Sally,' she said tautly. 'Dinner will be ready in about five minutes.'

She tried not to hurry from the room, but she knew she had not succeeded in hiding her nervous reactions—from her sister or from David Griffiths.

In the kitchen she closed the door and leaned against it, waiting until her pounding heart had settled to its normal steady rate. Damn the man. In the house for two minutes, and already he had disrupted her planned composure, completely disconcerted her.

For a moment in there, as he'd held her, steadied her after her trip, she'd thought he was going to kiss her. But the thing that made her even more uneasy was the fact that, instead of withdrawing at once, she had remained where she was, totally mesmerised by those eyes of his. He must have thought she was willing to let him . . . If Sally hadn't . . .

At this point she banished her disjointed imaginings and made herself concentrate on serving up. She was not going to let him ruin the results of her labours.

'I gather you've done the cooking tonight,' Griff said as she came in with the first of the dishes. He and Sally were already seated at the table, deep in conversation. But at Jodi's appearance he stood up. 'I'm flattered,' he went on. 'I——'

'You needn't be,' she said hastily. And then, because it wasn't natural to her to be rude, she felt bound to qualify her remark. 'This is merely the first day of a new regime. From now on I'll be cooking all the meals. Sally needs to rest more.'

Her sister's eyebrows rose at this statement, but to Jodi's relief she did not contradict it. The nerve of the man! Jodi fumed as she set his plate in front of him. Even supposing it were true, *he* had no call to assume that she had put herself out especially to please him.

But David Griffiths was not abashed by her disclaimer. 'My lucky day, then—if your cooking is as splendid as everything else about you.' And Jodi felt the colour warm her cheeks. But before she could think of a reply, he went on, 'Except for your attitude towards me. That leaves a lot to be desired, don't you think? But that can be remedied, I'm sure. I know, deep down, you like me.' And he smiled, green eyes dancing, his mobile mouth inviting her to respond in kind.

Sally spluttered over her soup, but after a swift glance at her sister's tense expression decided to mount a rescue operation.

'Tell me, Griff, have you always worked for the family firm?' she asked.

'Since I came down from university, yes. I've been managing an overseas branch until just recently. I rejoined the Oxford Street branch just six months ago. As Jodi's probably told you, I'm the managing director. But I take a particular interest in the fashion department. It's an area where I feel we need to expand.'

'Jodi's in fashion too,' Sally told him, sounding pleased at the coincidence. 'She has her own boutique.'

'A joint partnership,' Jodi amended, and then, faintly sarcastic, 'only a modest enterprise, of course, compared with the might of Griffiths.'

He nodded. 'Well, we all have to start somewhere,' he said kindly.

It was her own fault for inviting the riposte, but the deliberate note of patronage in his tone, the mocking gleam in his eye, set her teeth on edge, but there was nothing she could say. In actual fact her boutique had begun to earn quite a reputation for itself, having a loyal following, and there had been several offers from larger enterprises to buy her and Lucinda out.

But at least Sally's attempt at redirecting the conversation had succeeded, and throughout the rest of the meal her sister continued to draw Griff out on the subject of his work.

Not that he needed much encouragement to talk. He spoke rapidly, fluently. He was an interesting conversationalist, his speech loaded with witty remarks and amusing anecdotes about life in a big department store. Once or twice Jodi found herself laughing aloud, until a sobering thought occurred to her.

No doubt some future recipient of his confidences would hear the one about their confrontation in the grotto.

They had just settled down in the sitting-room with their after-dinner coffee when a wail from upstairs brought Sally to her feet.

'I'll go,' Jodi said hastily, rising too. But Sally waved her back.

'It'd better be me. I've been expecting this. I think she's after another tooth.'

Left alone with David Griffiths in a room only softly lit by background lamps and firelight, Jodi knew a distinct sense of unease. It worried her, his solidity, his surprising attractiveness, the fact that she couldn't look at him without feeling this disturbing internal response.

She was aware that he was looking at her, but she steadfastly refused to meet his gaze, keeping her head averted so that her face was in shadow to him.

'I don't bite, you know,' he said suddenly, breaking the tense little silence. 'So you needn't sit there looking as if you've been left alone with the family Rottweiler.'

Despite her inner tension an involuntary chuckle escaped her.

'That's better,' he said approvingly. 'You're beautiful whatever your expression, but a smile brings life and warmth to the picture. You know,' he added, rising from his armchair and walking towards her, 'yours is a very unusual beauty—quite new in my experience.'

And he was probably very experienced, Jodi thought. He looked the sort to have had a string of

women in his life. She stiffened her wavering resistance with the thought that he was probably the
perennial 'love 'em and leave 'em' bachelor.

He sat down beside her on the settee, the only seat
that had been left to her as they gathered about the
blazing open fire.

Jodi shifted uneasily, but he checked her instinctive
movement towards flight.

'Don't go,' he said softly, his hand on her arm de-
taining her. 'Don't run away from me. Let me look
at you properly. Until now I've only had fleeting
glimpses—tantalising, unsatisfying, like a mirage in
the desert to a thirsty man.'

He certainly had a way with words, Jodi thought.
But then his job had probably programmed him to
compliment women so that they felt good. For herself
she scorned the ploy of telling her customers they
looked marvellous in what, patently, did not suit them.
She had a great respect for truth.

But then all coherent thought left her as his hand
grasped her chin, turning her face towards him so that
the flickering firelight illuminated it for him. He
leaned forward, studying her, the movement bringing
him too close. He was invading her personal space.
And yet, as she had already had occasion to realise,
it was not a distasteful experience, as it could be with
some people.

'Yes, unusual,' he said again, 'a lovely, wistful,
haunting beauty. At least, it's haunted me, from the
first moment I saw you.'

'Even when you thought I was a rabble-rouser?'
she couldn't resist saying.

He smiled but refused to be diverted. 'And those
great grey eyes of yours—they give nothing away, no

clue to your thoughts. I get the feeling of remoteness. You're far away somewhere—elusive. Where are you, Jodi? Don't try to elude me.' He was husky now. 'Let me get to know you.'

'You're ... you're talking absolute rubbish,' Jodi said unsteadily. 'It ... it's just patter, isn't it? Sales talk. A line you take with women. I ... I don't care for it.'

'Perhaps because the right man hasn't said these things to you. Or because it wasn't said sincerely. You'll get used to it. You'll get used to me. You'll learn to like it, so that one day it will be a food you crave—food for your emotions. They're pretty well starved at present, aren't they?'

'No,' she denied. She pulled her chin free, dismayed at how long she had let him retain his grasp. She didn't like the implication that she was frustrated for the lack of a man in her life. 'I have plenty of men friends,' she told him.

It was true—men she had known for ages, with whom she was comfortable. She just wasn't looking for one closer relationship. Going out with a new man meant all the nonsensical aspects of dating, the giving and receiving of credentials, the feeling that you must present only your best side to the other person. And then—just when you were at ease with them, thought you knew them, trusted them—the let-down.

'We're all looking for someone,' he insisted, 'whether we admit it or not.'

'Speak for yourself,' she returned. 'Perhaps you don't know your own mind. I do.' Goodness, she wasn't usually so sharp. But it was his own fault, his refusal to accept her claim to lack of interest in him.

'Oh, I know my own mind,' he said, and with heavy significance, 'I also know what it's set on at the moment.'

Her heart gave a crazy flutter. 'Then I suggest,' she said pleasantly, 'that you remember the red tractor and prepare yourself for another disappointment.'

He was silent for so long that she thought she had finally quelled him, and her heart rate settled back to normal. But because he was still regarding her, the silence became oppressive.

She jumped up. 'For heaven's sake, will you stop staring at me?'

Because she had risen, he must also. But he ignored her complaint, slowly shaking his head, and she might have taken his words at face value but for the glint in his eyes.

'They say appearances are deceptive, and you don't look like a rabid feminist. So tell me, what have you got against men?'

Damn him! Why did he have this uncanny knack of continually putting her on the defensive? And why should she care if he thought her unappealingly unfeminine? But she did.

'Not men in general,' she explained. 'Just some. I particularly dislike the arrogant, presumptuous kind.'

He raised an eyebrow. 'And is that how you see me?'

'Do you blame me?' she asked plaintively. 'I've made it as clear as I can without being rude that I'm not interested. But you——'

'Oh, come on, Jodi, loosen up a bit. Life's too short. Why don't you let your hair down—literally?' he said, one hand reaching out to smooth her tight braids. 'The first time I saw you it was flowing free over your shoulders. The kind of hair a man would love to bury his face in.'

'Please,' she begged, aware that the dreaded weakness was afflicting her knees. 'Don't, I——'

'We could have fun together, you and I,' Griff said. 'Don't tell me you haven't a sense of fun somewhere, hidden underneath all that outraged dignity. Because I won't believe it, not having met your sister.'

'Of course I have. But I don't like being made a fool of.'

'Is that what you think I'm doing?' he said softly, peering into her face. 'Yes, I really believe you do think that. But you're wrong, you know. I really want to get to know you, Jodi. Maybe it's just that we got off on the wrong foot?' He reached for her hand, taking it in a warm clasp. 'Maybe we should start over?'

'I... look,' she said hastily, trying and failing to release her hand, trying and failing to appear quite calm and unflustered. 'I have to make you understand, have to make you see that...whatever you may think you want, I don't——'

'Still running away,' he sighed. 'Look, Jodi, I don't think, I know. But we needn't be anything more than two people enjoying each other's company—if that's the way you'd prefer it. And I can guarantee you an enjoyable time, if you do possess that sense of fun you lay claim to.'

Jodi was spared the necessity of answering by Sally's return. But she was not quick enough to retrieve her hand, and in consequence received a speculative look from her sister.

'Tanya's asleep, thank goodness.' Sally sank down into her chair, stifling a yawn. 'Sorry I was gone so long. I must have dropped off for a moment myself.' And to David Griffiths, 'I hope Jodi's been looking after you.'

He smiled gravely. 'Perhaps not as adequately as I could have wished. But you're tired,' he said. 'I mustn't outstay my welcome,' a sidelong look at Jodi, 'if I haven't already. No, Sally, don't get up.' He bent over her and took her hand. 'Seriously, I've enjoyed my evening and I'd like to return your hospitality. May I take you both out for a meal some time?'

Sally smiled up at him. 'Thanks, but no, thanks. I'm not going out much at present—getting too close to D-Day. But do take Jodi. She——'

'I couldn't possibly,' Jodi said quickly. 'I'm here to keep you company. I——'

Lightly Sally disposed of her objection. 'I'm sure I can get someone to come in for one evening.' To Griff she explained, 'It's only so there's someone to stay with the children when I go into labour.'

'Well, Jodi?' He was looking at her questioningly.

It wasn't fair. He shouldn't be able to exert such potent persuasion. And it was irritating that she, who had been so determined not to succumb, was affected by that potency. David Griffiths could be very dangerous, she realised. He was a man determined to have his own way where she was concerned.

Even so, 'All right,' she found herself saying. It was feeble of her to capitulate. And immediately, to herself, she defended her acquiescence by telling herself he was quite capable of standing there until she did agree and it was time Sally got to bed.

* * *

'And what are you looking so smug about?' she demanded of her sister as the front door closed behind him.

'Because I was right about him. He is nice. Probably one of the nicest men we've ever met.'

'Nice?' Jodi screwed up her nose. Despite her own reluctance to admit his attractions, she would have thought Sally could do better than that overworked adjective.

'Yes, and not boring nice. I suspect he could never be boring. And he's really keen on you, Jodi—anyone could see that.'

'All the more reason not to get involved.'

'Jodi Knight!'

Jodi stared at her sister, for Sally's tone was unusually sharp.

'I could shake you sometimes,' Sally went on. 'There you are, with dozens of dishy men falling over themselves to be with you. Along comes the dishiest of them all, and all you do is give him the cold shoulder. Meanwhile there's me, only needing one man to be with me—and what do I get?' Her voice cracked ominously, and Jodi flew to her side.

'Oh, Sal, I wish I could do something to help. Why couldn't you have met someone who'd be around all the time? Someone like Griff. He's so...' She stopped short, realising what she had said, what she had almost given away. 'Well, anyway,' she went on quickly before her sister could comment, 'you don't deserve all the hassle you get.'

Griff telephoned two days later—just as Jodi was beginning to wonder if he'd thought better of his campaign. She wasn't in the habit of finding herself so preoccupied with a man, and it bothered her.

'Oh, it's you!' she said, then was immediately annoyed with herself for sounding piqued that he'd waited this long to get in touch with her.

'Can you make dinner tonight?' he asked, and, 'I'll pick you up at eight.' Then, 'Do you like dancing? I thought—after we'd eaten——'

'Oh, I can't stay out that long,' Jodi said quickly. Dancing was altogether too intimate an activity. 'Just in case Sally——'

'Oh, that's easily taken care of.' With which cryptic remark he rang off.

His meaning was made clear when he arrived that evening.

'Eight o'clock on the dot,' he said as she opened the door. 'See how keen I am to make a good impression? Especially as Mrs Monkton will tell you I'm not the most punctual of men as a rule.' And she saw that he was accompanied by a middle-aged woman whom he introduced as his secretary. 'Mrs Monkton is willing to stay with your sister as long as necessary,' he told Jodi after introductions had been performed and Mrs Monkton was chatting with Sally, 'and she has her own transport for afterwards.'

His blithe assumption that his arrangements would be immediately acceptable left Jodi breathless. 'You——' she began, but was not allowed to continue.

'Don't bother to thank me,' he said cheerfully. 'I've done it as much for Aggie's sake as much as anyone's. She's been a widow for some years now, and while her work occupies her days, her evenings I suspect are sometimes lonely.'

It was impossible to maintain her indignation in the face of his obvious, good-natured concern for his secretary. 'Oh, well,' she muttered, 'so long as Sally doesn't mind.'

She could see that the subject was already dismissed as far as he was concerned. Instead his full concentration was upon her, those glittering green eyes making a long, slow assessment.

'You look absolutely stunning,' he said huskily, and Jodi was torn between gratification and the wish that she hadn't taken quite such obvious pains with her appearance.

The dress, for a start—one of her own creations—struck her now as being altogether too provocative, with its clinging lines and deep neckline—facts of which Griff's eyes proclaimed him all too aware. He might think—obviously did think—she had dressed to allure. And he—as his words revealed—seemed poised to take advantage of the fact.

'Thank you,' she said stiltedly.

He misread her conflicting emotions and his expression became wry, his words making her feel guilty of a churlishness she had not intended. 'Am I not even allowed to compliment you?'

'I'm...I'm sorry, I didn't mean to sound...I'm afraid I'm too used to people who say one thing but mean another.'

'For people read men?' he enquired, and, as she nodded, 'I meant exactly what I said—no more, no less. One thing I pride myself on is a strict regard for truth. I said you looked stunning, and you do. Can't you see how stunned I look?'

As he feigned the reaction he described, Jodi couldn't repress a chuckle. 'I'm sorry,' she said again, but this time she meant it. He had been totally honest with her right from the start. 'Mr Griffiths, I——'

'Oh, come on. Surely by now you could at least use my first name? Though I'd prefer it if you called me Griff. I've never felt like a David, somehow.'

'Why's that?' a diverted Jodi asked. It had never occurred to her to wonder if her name fitted her.

'Too staid an image,' he said promptly. 'I have an uncle David—he's eighty now, but he's always seemed incredibly old even when I was a boy.'

'No one,' she agreed feelingly, 'could ever accuse you of being staid.'

'So is it to be Griff, then?' And as she nodded, 'Good!' His satisfaction expressed itself in a warm clasp of her arm. 'That's progress of a sort.'

Jodi had not formed any preconceived ideas of where Griff would take her this evening. Which was probably just as well. For she could never have predicted the reality.

No intimate dimly lit haute cuisine restaurant with a pocket-handkerchief floor upon which dancing could only be a shuffling excuse for proximity. Instead a large complex which as well as its restaurant boasted leisure facilities and an enormous ballroom where an energetic disco was in progress. And Jodi was torn between relief and something oddly like disappointment when the closest they ever came in the dance was an arm's length.

'I must say,' she confessed with breathless laughter, during a brief intermission, 'I wouldn't have expected this to be your scene.'

'Why not? You don't object, I hope?' She got the impression that, if she had, he would have been prepared to whisk her away elsewhere. And as she shook her head, 'For my own part I enjoy any form of dancing. I like variety. But I thought this...' he indicated the still wildly gyrating couples, 'would be a safer bet for our first date.'

'Safer?' Jodi asked unwarily.

'Yes,' he smiled, and immediately she knew something embarrassing was coming. 'I know my own weaknesses, and to hold you close on the dance-floor would be altogether too much for my self-control.'

As the car halted outside the Hampstead house, Griff turned towards Jodi, his hands coming up to cup her face.

'Whoa, there,' he admonished her as she tried to jerk away. 'This is only by way of thanking you for this evening. I've really enjoyed myself.'

So had she, she realised, though wild horses wouldn't drag so revealing an admission from her.

He lowered his head, slowly, as though he were afraid of alarming her—just far enough for his lips to brush against hers.

The feelings that washed over her, from even so slight a contact, were incredibly erotic, tiny shivers of pleasure making her body throb as though from a series of electric shocks.

He was aware of his effect on her—she sensed that. And she would have expected him to follow up the advantage he had gained. But to her surprise he released her.

'Goodnight, Jodi,' he said.

He did not even suggest escorting her to the door, though she was aware that the car waited until she was safely inside.

Her legs were shaking as she made for the stairs. She was the one who had wanted that kiss to continue, to deepen. It was totally illogical, making a farce of all her earlier claims to uninterest in David Griffiths.

'Jodi?' Sally's voice from the sitting-room reminded her that she had not announced her return. Reluctantly, she turned away from the stairs. She did not feel like encountering her sister's shrewd gaze right now.

'Everything all right? Did you enjoy yourself?' Sally looked tired, but Jodi guessed her sister had no intention of succumbing to her fatigue until her curiosity was satisfied.

But, aware of Griff's secretary now collecting up her coat and gloves, Jodi was not about to say more than a formal, 'Yes, thank you.'

'Right! Give!'

If Jodi thought she had evaded the inquisition she was much mistaken. Within minutes of the front door closing behind Mrs Monkton, Sally was coming into her sister's bedroom.

'Time you were asleep,' Jodi said pointedly. 'Mrs Monkton was supposed to be babysitting you. You didn't have to sit up with her.'

'I didn't like to leave her alone,' Sally explained. 'Besides, she's good company. And you should just hear her sing Griff's praises. He sounds a thoroughly decent, caring man. So,' she plumped down on the edge of Jodi's bed, 'how did it go?'

Jodi was evasive. 'Just as you'd expect any dinner date to go. We ate, talked, danced a little.'

'Has he kissed you yet?' Sally was impatient to know, and despite herself Jodi chuckled, irresistibly reminded of their teenage years, when they had sat up into the small hours, comparing notes. Even then there had been a marked difference in their attitudes.

Sally, the romantic, the born homemaker, couldn't wait to be first engaged and then married, trying her first name over in conjunction with the surname of the current boyfriend, whereas Jodi had always kept her relationships light, openly declaring that she did not intend to marry until she was at least thirty.

'I want to make something of myself first—be a real person, not just somebody's wife.' And ever since her experience with Rodney she had been even more determined to fend off even the most persistent of male advances.

'You couldn't really call it a kiss,' she said now. 'Just a token brush of lips.'

Maybe, an inner voice said, but if just a 'token brush' could make her feel that way, what havoc could a full-blooded kiss wreak upon her susceptibilities?

CHAPTER THREE

'So, when's your next date?' Sally asked. And accusingly, at Jodi's blank expression, 'You mean you don't know? You haven't fixed anything?'

Until Sally fired her questions it simply hadn't occurred to Jodi. But now she realised Griff hadn't said anything about seeing her again. Why? Not that it mattered, she told herself hastily. But it did seem odd, after his initial eagerness. Perhaps he was one of those men who enjoyed the chase but lost interest once the quarry was caught. Somehow this thought was not a pleasant one.

To Sally she said carelessly, 'I don't suppose I *will* see him again. I never had any intention of this becoming a regular thing.' Nevertheless an inexplicable shiver scudded through her—a shiver she excused by blaming the weather. 'It's cold enough out there for snow. Perhaps we'll have a white Christmas. How Robin would love that!'

She was right about one thing—the snow. Sleeping less soundly than usual—if thoughts of Griff did not keep her awake he appeared in her dreams instead—she woke about five-thirty. A strange white light was streaming in through a gap in her curtains. The room felt unusually cold and, shivering, she got up to investigate.

Moonlight, reflecting off a heavy fall of snow, made the Hampstead street an old-fashioned scene from a

Christmas card. Pristinely white, the snow was thickly mounded on roofs and settled in corners of windows. Only a coach and horses and a plump robin were needed to complete the picture.

Fat wet flakes were still falling and the air felt icy. Shuddering, Jodi shut the window, closed the curtains and scrambled back beneath the duvet.

It seemed only seconds later that she started up in the bed, wondering what sudden noise had woken her. It came again—a heavy thud that rattled the windowpane.

Snow sliding off the roof? A bit too soon, surely, for a thaw to be setting in? As she got out of bed once more a glance at her watch told her it was only six o'clock.

She opened the curtains—then jumped back in alarm as something struck the window close to her face. Then she realised what it was. A snowball. Who on earth . . . ? Cautiously she opened the window and peered out into the dark garden, to see a tall figure silhouetted against the white background. She might have known.

'At last!' Griff's familiar voice said. 'I thought I'd have to do a Romeo and climb up to your balcony.'

'I haven't got a balcony,' she pointed out. 'And what on earth are you doing here at this ungodly hour of the morning? How did you know this was my room?'

'Observation. And I often get up at this time,' he said cheerfully. 'I love mornings, especially mornings like this, don't you?'

'Not particularly,' Jodi said, 'and not at this time of year.' The icy atmosphere was penetrating even her warmly practical pyjamas—not the most glamorous night attire to be seen in. She made to withdraw.

'Hang on, Juliet!' Griff shouted. 'Don't go. How soon can you be ready?'

'Ready for what?'

'A brisk walk in the snow. Don't you think there's something very satisfying, very exciting about virgin territory, being the first person to set foot on a stretch of unmarked——'

'Go away!' Jodi said, half laughing, half serious. 'I'm not getting up for at least another two hours.'

'Slugabed!' he accused. 'In another two hours all this will be slush, ruined by milkmen, paper boys and postmen. Come on! If you don't,' he threatened, 'I shall sing an aria under your window, and . . .' darkly '. . . your neighbours might not appreciate that.'

The threatened laughter escaped her. Suddenly the morning air did not seem quite as cold. A walk in the snow sounded inviting. But her capitulation must not seem too total.

'Since it seems I'm not to get any more sleep,' she grumbled.

'Good. How long will you be?'

'Ten minutes.'

'Make it five.'

She made him wait nearly fifteen before she opened the front door. He wasn't going to have it all his own way.

Despite the chilly morning the large hand that grasped hers and pulled her rapidly down the path was as warm as toast. Her flesh tingled at the contact. At the front gate she stopped, puzzled.

'Where's your car?' she queried.

'At my friend's house. I stayed there overnight. In the village, remember?'

'Where are we going?'

'Up to the Heath.'

'You're mad,' she told him exasperatedly, 'do you know that?'

'If I am it's your fault. I've been affected with a kind of madness from the first moment I saw you.' He said it so casually that Jodi did not feel threatened, and she responded in kind.

'I've a feeling the insanity goes back a lot further than that.'

The day was lighter now, and the vast rugged expanse of Heath was as virginally, sparklingly white as Griff could desire. The only tracks upon its satisfyingly crunchy surface were the spiky triangular footmarks left by bird life.

The sight of all that unblemished snow was an irresistible invitation, and Jodi succumbed to sudden impulse.

'Now,' she said, 'I'm about to get my revenge for being woken up at such an unearthly hour.' With that she began to scoop up handfuls of the icy snow. She hadn't indulged in a snowball fight since childhood. In those days, something of a tomboy, she had been a deadly shot. Had she lost the knack?

In a way this was a kind of test. How Griff responded to the challenge would tell her much about his personality.

He did not disappoint her. Soon the snowballs were whizzing back and forth, most of them finding their target, for Griff was as adept as she. It was exhilarating exercise. But at last, laughing and breathless, Jodi called a halt.

'I'm exhausted. And I really must get back, to help with the children's breakfast.'

Griff looked at his watch. 'And I must get into town.'

'You're not driving in town, not in this?' she asked, surprised to feel a tinge of anxiety on his behalf.

'No, I'll take the Underground.'

'Even so,' she pointed out, 'you're going to be late.' Wickedly, 'But I suppose management can get away with that.'

'For that snide remark,' Griff threatened, 'you deserve to be severely punished.'

'No more snowballs,' Jodi begged. 'I'm wet enough.'

'You started it,' he pointed out. 'But actually I had something warmer in mind.' And before she realised what he was about, his arms were about her.

She could have fought free of him. But she didn't.

His mouth was as cold as hers, but as their lips touched, clung, lingered, a sweet warmth generated between them.

Jodi shivered, but not from the wintry cold this time. Now she did draw away, disturbed by conflicting feelings. The strange inner pulsings of her body told her she had wanted the kiss to continue. But her independent, self-reliant nature felt subtly endangered.

Griff was watching her with a quizzical expression, and she hoped her inner turmoil was not written on her face. She had thought herself used to his height, but now she was very much aware of him towering over her.

'I wish I could stay—all day,' he said, 'but unfortunately——'

'It's just as well,' she told him, crushing back her own regret that this interlude was over. 'I haven't time to play childish games all day. I——'

'Did the last few moments come under the heading of childish games?' he wanted to know.

'Well, of course! It was just part of the fun, not meant to be taken seriously.' It seemed very important to assert that, not just for his benefit but for her own.

'I see.' Again that searching look. But he said no more, and they began the long trudge back.

To break the silence which had fallen, Jodi asked him, 'Do you make a habit of arriving unexpectedly on people's doorsteps?'

'Only when I want to catch someone off her guard. Someone,' he added with heavy significance, 'who persists in refusing to take me seriously.'

Which perhaps was why, she thought—after he had left her outside Sally's house—once again he hadn't arranged any future meetings. No doubt she could expect him to arrive, as always, out of the blue. And next time she mustn't allow herself to be so easily persuaded. Correction—she mustn't be persuaded at all.

In the past she had always been able to discourage even the most ardently persistent men. Which was why it puzzled her that she had already accorded Griff far more liberties than she would have dreamed possible two weeks ago. She needed time, that was all, to shore up her defences, to re-establish a safe distance between herself and David Griffiths.

Which perhaps explained the edgy way she jumped every time the telephone rang or someone came to the door. She couldn't believe that she was actually nervous. She didn't actually care whether he reap-

peared or not, did she? She, Jodi, whom some re-
jected men had dubbed icy and uncaring? No, it wasn't
possible. It mustn't be. She wasn't going to get hurt
again.

This uncharacteristic behaviour caused her sister
much smug satisfaction. 'I knew, right from the start,'
she said, 'that Griff was going to be different from
all the others.'

'Different?' Jodi demanded suspiciously. If Sally
thought he was going to succeed where others had
failed . . .

'He's a much stronger character,' Sally explained.
'The others all gave up on you too easily.'

'Rubbish. They were just being realistic. They knew
I didn't intend to take them seriously. Well, I don't
take Griff seriously either.'

'I'm not so sure,' Sally said cryptically. 'I know
you've often said, if you ever got married, it wouldn't
be until you were thirty. May I point out that that
happy event isn't too far distant?'

'Have a heart!' Jodi laughed. 'I've got another five
years.'

Sally shook her head. 'I might have believed that
once. But now that Griff has come along, I reckon
your days of being fancy-free are numbered. Just
think,' she mused, 'if you were to marry Griff you
wouldn't need Lucinda as a partner any more or have
to worry about finances. You'd have a wealthy
husband to stake you.'

Jodi stared at her in disbelief. 'Sally! You know me
better than that,' she protested. 'Even if I were to
marry—marry anyone, I mean,' she added hastily,
'I'm not necessarily talking about Griff—I'd want to

be responsible for my own business. I wouldn't want to be like Lucinda, just playing at it.'

This conversation reminded Jodi that it was about time she visited the boutique to see that all was well with her business. Friday morning, with Robin at playgroup, seemed a safe day to leave her sister for a few hours.

The trains into the West End were claustrophobically crowded with pre-Christmas shoppers, and most of the way she had to stand. Consequently she was feeling tired and irritable by the time she reached Oxford Street, and the news she received at the boutique did nothing to improve her mood.

'Thank goodness you've come in today!' Betty, one of the assistants, greeted her with palpable relief. 'If you hadn't I was going to telephone later.' She held out a letter. 'This came this morning, and you did say to open all mail.'

Jodi nodded and swiftly perused the few lines. The letter was from Lucinda, and it told her little more than she had already suspected. Her partner was tired of 'playing at shops'. She had met up with—to use her words—'a dishy ski instructor' and intended to stay in Switzerland indefinitely.

But it was the final paragraph of the letter which had so dismayed Betty.

I'd suggest that you buy me out, but there doesn't seem to be much point really. Daddy tells me Goodbodys are selling out to a bigger concern, and he reckons the new owners won't renew our lease.

'Have you heard anything about this?' Jodi asked the two girls.

'Not a thing. There haven't been any "For Sale" signs on Goodbodys' store. What will you do?' Obviously the girls were anxious about their own position, and Jodi didn't blame them.

'I'll ring Lucinda's father first. If he doesn't know any more I'll get in touch with Goodbodys' solicitors.'

Neither phone call had proved satisfactory, and Jodi seethed as she made the journey back to Hampstead.

Lucinda's father had been sympathetic, but now that his daughter was no longer involved in the enterprise he did not seem very concerned. Nor could he tell her any more about the rumoured takeover.

The solicitors, when she finally managed to get through on an irritatingly busy line, were evasive. The deal had not yet been concluded. They were not empowered to reveal any information as yet. She would be advised in due course as to the name of her new landlords and their future intentions about their property, but this information was unlikely to be forthcoming until the New Year.

None of this was very reassuring. The original lease on the shop was nearing the end of its run, and a new owner might not see fit to renew it. The more she thought about it, the more Jodi's anxiety and sense of frustration increased. Her impatient, impulsive nature meant that she had never been very good at waiting. Anticipation of good news was barely endurable, but waiting for bad news...

Despite all Sally's attempts at optimism, Jodi's irritable mood persisted into the weekend, and she was in no better frame of mind on Sunday morning when the doorbell rang and she was the only one available to answer it.

Sally, unusually for her, was lying in. Tanya, a placid baby, was still obligingly asleep in the cot beside her. But there was no prospect of a rest for Jodi, with a wide-awake and excited Robin begging her to help him make a snowman.

'When I've washed my hair and put some clothes on,' she kept saying in reply to his insistent pleas.

So she was still in her dressing-gown with her long hair damp about her shoulders.

'Don't you ever let the day get aired before you go making calls?' she demanded exasperatedly of Griff.

'I wanted to be sure of catching you,' he explained, stamping the snow from his shoes.

Jodi said sarcastically, 'Oh, you've caught me all right!' A gesture indicated her state of undress. She discovered she did not like him to find her looking so totally unglamorous—hair in rat's tails, not a vestige of make-up. 'What's so important that you mustn't miss me?'

'Our anniversary, of course.' He was in the hallway now, and Jodi backed away from him. She felt much too vulnerable without what Sally called her armour and warpaint.

She must have misheard him. 'Our what?' she echoed.

He grinned. 'Our anniversary—remember? Two weekends ago—the first time we met. I thought we should celebrate.'

'What utter nonsense,' Jodi said faintly. 'Two weeks is nothing, and, besides, we——'

'Two weeks can be nothing—or everything,' he said significantly, 'depending on your point of view and what use you make of the time.'

Jodi couldn't resist the riposte. 'Well, you're wasting yours,' she told him. But even to her own ears her tone lacked its usual conviction.

'Oh, I wouldn't say that. I think we've made quite a bit of progress in our relationship.'

'We don't have a relationship. And now, if you don't mind, I have things to do, including getting dressed. It's too cold to stand around arguing.'

'Fine,' to her consternation he moved towards the living-room, 'I can wait.'

'Auntie Jodi,' Robin, who had been silent until now, decided to renew his claim to her attention, 'are we going to make a snowman?'

'Yes, of course, darling. Get your hat and coat and your wellies. I won't be long. As you can see,' she told Griff, 'I have a previous engagement.'

When she came downstairs again ten minutes later there was no sign either of Robin or of Griff. But squeals of merriment from the back garden told her where they were, and with a resigned sigh she went to find them.

The snowman was already well under construction and the two architects had taken time out for a snowball fight.

'Uncle Griff said we'd better leave a bit for you to do,' Robin informed her kindly.

'Oh, did he?' So it was Uncle Griff now, was it? Whose idea had that been? She thought she could guess. And the look on Griff's face confirmed it.

'I've never had a nephew,' he explained.

'You don't have one now,' quickly she deflated his pretensions. '"Uncle" in your case is only a courtesy title Sally insists on. She doesn't like to hear children calling adults by their first name.' She looked at him consideringly. 'Frankly,' she said, 'I'm surprised you don't have children of your own by now.'

'You think I'd make a good father?' He sounded pleased at a compliment that had not been paid nor intended. Or had it?

'I wouldn't know about that, would I?' Jodi said quickly. 'I just meant it's unusual for a man of your age to be unmarried.'

Griff was suddenly grave. 'I was married once.'

'Oh?' Impossible to disguise her curiosity. Nor could she deny, to herself—though of course it was totally illogical—that it gave her an unpleasant feeling to discover there had been another woman in Griff's life—such an important relationship.

'She died,' he told her flatly, 'in a road accident— on Christmas Eve, five years ago.'

'I'm sorry.' Jodi was shocked by the strength of her feelings, the compassion that swept through her, making her want to put her arms about him and banish that bleak look from his eyes. 'How long were you——?'

'Four years.' And, grimly, 'Not long, is it?'

Jodi shook her head. 'No—that's the trouble with loving someone. Despite what the romantics would have us believe, it isn't all undiluted happiness.'

He looked at her keenly. 'You speak from experience?'

'Not my own. But my parents' marriage ended in divorce. And I've seen what loving someone so much has done to Sally. She tries hard to hide it—and she'd never tell him—but she's utterly lost when Barry's not around. And worried sick in case anything happens to him.'

'In her case, though,' Griff suggested, 'the pleasure is obviously worth the pain?'

'Was it for you?' Jodi ventured to ask. 'Worth it, I mean?'

'Very much so.'

She looked at him wonderingly. 'So how can you be the way you are now? So...so normal.'

He shrugged. 'When it happens you think, "That's it. My life's over." But eventually you find you can't weep for ever. And June was a very unselfish person. She wouldn't have wanted me to be miserable for the rest of my days. And so...' the cloud passed from his face and his attractive smile broke through once more '...let's get on with life, shall we? You've got a snowman to finish,' he reminded her, 'and then we'll have our celebration.'

Somehow, in view of the sad little history he had just related, Jodi did not feel like quashing his suggestion.

'All right,' she said. 'What do you have in mind?'

'Lunch first. Then a walk. Then dinner. And dancing again.'

Jodi looked at him in dismay. This was more than she'd bargained for. 'But...I can't spend the whole day——' she began.

'Why not?'

'Sally...the children...I'm——'

'Not indispensable. I'm sure your sister would see it that way. She also seems to be a remarkably unselfish person. My Mrs M took to her straight away, said she'd be happy to keep her company any time. So——?'

'Well,' Jodi said slowly, 'if Sally doesn't mind and your secretary is available...'

'She is—I already checked. I'll let her know it's on.'
Griff headed for the house. Once again, Jodi realised,
with very little effort on his part, he had got his own
way.

Griff's idea of a celebratory lunch was to take her to
one of the village pubs—a popular haunt of media
personalities—and for the first part of their meal Jodi
was diverted by Griff's nodding acquaintance with so
many of them.

'Good customers at Griffiths Brothers, most of
them,' he explained.

As the bar slowly emptied he still seemed disposed
to linger, turning the conversation towards more personal topics.

'You seemed surprised that I wasn't married, and
now you know why. But what about you? Why haven't
you met Mr Right? As my mother used to say, "Until
now, of course",' he added pointedly.

Jodi ignored the rider. 'Principally because I haven't
been looking. I've never been one to assess every man
I meet as husband material.'

'No boyfriends? I can't believe that. Not with your
face and figure.' His gaze was frankly admiring.

Jodi wished she didn't blush so easily. 'Plenty, but
none of them serious.'

'They weren't serious or you weren't?'

'I wasn't.'

'And all because of your parents' unhappy marriage? Or,' shrewdly, 'have you been hurt by
someone?'

'Both,' she said briefly. She didn't intend to discuss
Rodney with Griff. 'But it's also because I put a great

value on my independence. I like to be able to come
and go as I like, with no one quizzing me all the time.'

'Independence may be all very well when you're
young,' Griff said, 'but what about when you're
older? Or when things go wrong? You could be very
lonely.'

'I'm not saying I'll never get married. I——'

'The longer you leave it the less likely it is,' he
pointed out. 'You may find all the men of your age
already spoken for.'

'Surely that isn't a very good reason for getting
married?' Jodi asked humorously. 'It's like shopping
at the January sales just for the sake of it and ending
up with something you don't really want or need.'

A wry smile rewarded her analogy. 'I'm not sure,'
he said, 'that I relish being likened to surplus
merchandise.'

'But we're not talking about you,' she said quickly.
Goodness, for all his comments about 'Mr Right', she
didn't want to sound as if she thought he was pro-
posing marriage!

But he chose to see quite the opposite meaning. 'Oh,
good!' He reached across the table and took her hand.
'So you think I might be a bargain?'

Firmly she withdrew her hand. 'I don't think of
you either way. How on earth did we get into such a
ridiculous conversation?'

'I am in the business of selling, after all,' he reminded her. 'You can't blame me for trying to sell
myself.'

'Well, I'm not buying at present. So could we please
change the subject.'

'Right!' He downed the rest of his drink in one
swallow. 'Let's go for that walk. I thought we'd go
up on the Heath again.' And, with a return to the

wicked innuendo that was never very far away, 'Somehow you seem much more approachable out of doors.'

Which made Jodi resolve immediately to keep her distance from him. There was no way she was going to allow him to repeat that kiss, with its disturbing effect upon her.

Their walk was unlike any she had ever taken. Walking for walking's sake had never really appealed to her. But with Griff it was impossible to be bored.

She had never known anyone, man or woman, who could keep up such a constant flow of lively conversation covering so many topics, ranging from the serious or tragic to the comical. One moment his anecdotes had her on the verge of tears, the next helpless with laughter. Never before had anyone stirred her to such depths and heights of emotion.

It was, she conceded, a dangerous knack he had, making it difficult to maintain her usual aloofness, her policy of non-involvement.

Instead, as he related his stories, many of them personal experiences, she felt as though she herself was being caught up in his life, sharing it, knowing and liking him better every moment.

And when, in a moment of sudden exuberance, he took her hand and made her run with him over the snowy Heath, she went unresistingly, breathless not only with the exertion but with the laughter of pure enjoyment.

When at last they came to a halt by a cluster of trees, she was glowing with the exhilarating exercise, her cheeks—and alas, her nose, as Griff pointed out— pinkened by the cold air.

He seemed to find the rosiness of her face a matter for closer inspection, cupping it in his gloved hands. And, as she tensed, 'You're running scared, aren't you?' he said. 'But you needn't be frightened of me, Jodi,' and before she could think of an answer or a way of evading him, he had her in his arms.

'Griff...no...I...' Nervously she ran her tongue over cold lips that were also, suddenly, dry.

'Jodi, Jodi! Relax!' It was the softest of murmurs. The green eyes were twin flames now, their expression making her catch her breath. And then his mouth came down firmly on hers, a kiss so unlike his previous ones that it took her totally by surprise. It was fierce, impassioned, an unexpectedly sensual onslaught, his mouth wide and moist on hers, his tongue moving between her lips as he pulled her hard up against him.

But as suddenly as he'd grabbed her, he released her—before she was ready for him to do so. She'd been quite happy, she realised, to be in his arms.

'Snow-madness,' he said, but his voice was husky and the fire still lingered in his eyes.

It seemed he didn't want the kiss taken seriously, so she nodded. But inwardly she was shaking. She had been kissed many times by different men, but she couldn't remember even one of them affecting her like this.

Already she was regretting her promise to spend the whole day—and evening—with him. She wished she could cry off their dinner date—and the dancing. But somehow she knew Griff would see this as an admission that she was 'running scared', as he'd put it, see it as an incentive maybe to press home his advantage.

No, what she must do was play it cool, hold him at arm's length for the rest of the day and then tell him, politely but firmly, that she didn't wish to see him again.

During the necessary interval for them both to change into evening wear, she would rehearse the cool little speech she would make.

Holding Griff at arm's length might have been possible if he had decided to take her disco dancing again. But she might have known he wouldn't be so predictable.

He took her to a hotel this time. The head waiter ushered them towards a table for two, dimly lit and discreetly screened from general view—by living plants, not the plastic substitutes Jodi abominated. There was a pleasant atmosphere about the place, but she would have felt more at ease in a less intimate situation.

'Well?' Griff said as soon as they were seated. He was obviously awaiting her approval.

'Very select,' she said drily. 'Though not quite what I expected after last time.'

'Variety is the spice of life,' he quoted. 'Don't you think so? In activities as well as in friendship?'

He liked variety in his friendships? That was a point worth remembering, Jodi thought, surprised at the unease it caused her.

'And the dance-floor,' she said, eyeing the minute, polished wood area apprehensively, 'wouldn't make a decent dining table.'

'I rather fancied displaying my versatility.' That wicked gleam was there in his eyes again as he went on, 'And I thought you might prefer to be less energetic tonight. It would be a pity to dishevel all that glamorous poise.' He sounded as if he meant quite the opposite.

Jodi had been rather pleased with her own appearance, considering that it projected the coolly remote image she wished to maintain—blonde hair swept up elegantly around her head, the silvery gown echoing the colour of her eyes.

But, judging by Griff's expression, all her forethought did not seem to be having the desired effect, and, not without a little unease, she made a graceful acknowledgement of his compliment.

The hotel cuisine was excellent, but Jodi scarcely noticed what she ate. She was too vividly aware of what was to follow. It was ridiculous, a foolishness completely unlike her, but she was actually afraid of dancing with Griff. And as the meal advanced, she sought desperately for a way of prolonging it, putting off that inevitable moment when she would have to go into his arms.

Conversation—that was it. If she could only get him talking, relating more of his anecdotes.

'It occurs to me,' she said, 'that you've winkled out all kinds of personal details about my life. Yet I know very little about you. I know where you work, of course, that you're a widower. But that's about all. I don't know anything about your family background, your likes and dislikes, hobbies——'

'Whoa! Whoa!' Griff raised a hand. 'One thing at a time. Firstly, I know more about you because, until now, I've been more interested in you than you are in me. Is that about to change?'

Heavens, she'd given him the wrong idea altogether. 'We have to talk about something,' she pointed out.

'And you'd rather I talked about myself than paid you compliments, is that it?' Why did he have to be so damned shrewd? 'All right,' he went on before she could answer, 'I'll give you a brief résumé. I come from a large family—two brothers, four sisters. I'm the eldest. My brothers and sisters are all married. One brother's a doctor, the other is also with Griffiths as buildings manager—he's responsible for the purchase of properties and their maintenance, whereas I prefer to concentrate the merchandise and public relations side of the business. Hobbies? Badminton, swimming, reading. Foreign travel when I have time. And I like you,' he concluded with heavy significance.

Trust him to bring the conversation back to the personal. Not only that, but he had disposed in five minutes of a subject Jodi had hoped would take half an hour. She picked up on the one omission.

'No dislikes?'

He gave that scant consideration. 'On the whole I think I'm pretty tolerant. But I'll give you a short list, since you're so set on it. Loud-mouthed drunken men, bitchy women and...' here it came, she thought apprehensively, he had that look in his eyes '...and sitting still too long. Especially,' with a jerk of his head, 'when the dance-floor beckons and I have an attractive partner.'

She might have known the moment could not be deferred for ever. The small band was currently playing a popular waltz tune which in other circumstances would have had her feet tapping. Griff rose, holding out his hand to her.

As she had feared, the small floor, the number of dancers, gave him an excuse to draw her protectively

close. He was so large, so solid. So...so masculine.
She drew in a controlling breath.

Jodi was tall herself, but even so her cheek was only
on a level with a steadily beating heart. Her own, she
was aware, was behaving in a very erratic fashion.

She had danced with many men over the years.
Some she had liked, some she had disliked. But never
before had it been such an alarming experience. It
wasn't that she disliked Griff or that she found him
physically repellent. Far from it. He didn't smell of
stale tobacco or alcohol as many men did. His breath
was warmly sweet, fanning her temple.

Sexual attraction—she had to admit that was what
she found so alarming. But she didn't intend to give
in to it. She knew she was holding herself stiffly, and
he told her so.

'Relax, Jodi,' he murmured against her ear.

How could she relax when she was tensed as if for
flight, her defences, carefully erected and tended, now
in danger of crumbling. And all because of a man
she'd known for only two weeks.

'Happy anniversary,' he murmured in her ear, and,
'I wonder just how many years of them we'll be
celebrating?'

'The longest I've ever been out with any man,' she
felt compelled to tell him, 'was six months.'

'What was the secret of his success?' Griff enquired
drily.

'He was away a lot.'

He threw back his head and laughed aloud, pure
unrestrained amusement.

'What's so funny?' she demanded indignantly.

'You are. You never miss a chance to give me a set-
down or a warning. But ''the lady doth protest too

much, methinks".' He drew her closer, and as the pounding of her heart reached almost deafening levels, he delivered his *coup de grâce*. 'You're not as indifferent to me as you like to pretend. So you'd better get used to the idea, Jodi. I'm going to be around for much longer than six months. Much, much longer,' he repeated emphatically.

'You're...you're very sure of yourself, aren't you?' she said unsteadily. As a set-down it was a dismal failure, but it was all she could manage.

'Not always. Not about everything. But about this, about us—yes. From the first moment I saw you there was a sense of rightness, of belonging. You're going to belong to me, Jodi,' he murmured softly, 'one way or another.'

'Don't be so ridiculous,' she said faintly. One way or another? What did he mean by that, for goodness' sake? She would dearly love to know, but she wasn't going to give any credence to his statement by asking. 'I think it's time we went,' she added. And to her surprise he made no objections.

'I was just about to suggest the same thing. I thought dancing with you would be enough—for now. But it isn't.'

'What do you mean by that?' At once Jodi was wary, suspicious. But as the music came to an end just at that moment she had to wait for her answer.

It was not until they had retrieved their coats and Griff was seating her in his car that she had an opportunity to repeat the question. But by then she was afraid to do so. She'd had too much opportunity to think, to imagine his meaning for herself. Dealing with Griff was difficult enough without her imagination running riot.

He was unusually silent as they drove away from the hotel. But this did not reassure Jodi one little bit. The silence was crackling with tension.

'This isn't the way to Sally's house,' she said suddenly.

'I know.'

'Then where are we going?' And on a sudden rising note of panic, 'Where are you taking me?'

'Relax, Jodi,' he soothed. 'We're just making a little detour.'

They were in Hampstead village by now, and without warning he pulled up—outside one of the small picturesque old houses she had so often admired.

'Where? What——?' she began.

'My friend's house. I told you I knew someone in the village. I stayed here the other night.'

He was calling by to collect some belongings. Jodi went limp with relief. But the relief was shortlived.

'Come on, get out.' He was holding her door open, his voice edged with impatience. For some reason he must want her to meet his friends.

'It's a bit late for social calls,' she objected. But obediently she released her safety-belt.

'This isn't a social call. I don't pay social calls at half past one in the morning.' A hand on her elbow, he was hurrying her up the path, still slippery with tightly packed snow. He had his own key, she noticed bemusedly.

'Then why——?' They were inside now and he was removing her coat, shrugging off his own.

He took her arm again, ushering her into a living-room of remarkably fine proportions considering the deceptive exterior of the house. But Jodi was in no frame of mind to study the décor. Griff was closing curtains, switching on a gas fire, making himself thoroughly at home.

'Griff!' She said his name sharply, nerves giving the edge to her voice. 'Will you please tell me what we're doing here?'

CHAPTER FOUR

'I'LL tell you, yes.' Griff came towards Jodi and put his hands on her shoulders, holding her at arm's length, his eyes gravely studying her face. 'Until now, our meetings have been either in the open air, public places or under the eyes of your sister. We've hardly ever been entirely alone. And when we have it's been in sub-zero temperatures—hardly conducive to love-making. My friend is away overnight, and so——'

'Oh!' Jodi gasped, then shrugged off his hands and backed away. 'And you've brought me here because you think I'll let you... Of all the nerve...! Of all the high-handed, presumptuous... Well, you couldn't be more wrong!' She moved towards the door. 'Take me home at once,' she commanded, and, as he made no sign of complying, 'Then I'll walk, or call a taxi.'

'Jodi, don't you think you're over-reacting? I don't know precisely what you think I have in mind.' The green eyes were gently mocking now. 'Surely you know me well enough by now to know I'm not suddenly going to turn into a sex maniac!'

But she wasn't going to be disarmed this time by his insouciant humour.

'You've no right to bring me here like this—without consulting me... to assume——'

'Jodi, I'm assuming nothing.' Somehow he'd managed to interpose himself between her and the only means of escape. 'Good lord, woman, there are many degrees of lovemaking. Trust me. We won't go any faster or further than you permit.'

'Trust you?' she echoed. It was meant to be scornful, but her voice was shaking too much. 'I've never known you take no for an answer yet. And as to how far we go—you've gone far enough already. Please let me pass.'

'Not yet. Give me half an hour of your time, Jodi. Surely that's not too much to ask? If after that you still want to go home I'll take you.'

'And just how do you propose we spend that half-hour?' She had meant the words to sound defiant, but instead they came out in a hoarse, barely audible croak.

The intensity of his gaze seemed to span the gap between them as if he were already touching her. 'I'll show you. Come here,' he ordered softly.

Mutely she shook her head. If he thought he had only to beckon...

'Then I'll come to you.' The single step he took was enough. She turned to run. But there was nowhere to go.

His hands on her shoulders were gentle but firm as he turned her back to face him, then bent his head to brush a light kiss across her forehead. 'Jodi, Jodi, you don't have to be afraid of me.'

She wasn't, she realised. It was herself she feared most, these strange new reactions that no other man had ever managed to evoke.

Griff laid an arm about her waist, the other hand grasping and lifting her chin so that her lips could not refuse to meet his. The surge of physical desire was so sudden that it made her gasp aloud, so shaken that she could not have pulled free even if she'd wanted to. Instead, incredibly, she found herself clinging to Griff's broad shoulders, only dimly aware that he was drawing her towards the massive sofa, easily large enough to hold them both in comfort.

His hand cupped her face and his lips brushed hers again. 'We'll take it one step at a time,' he crooned softly against her mouth. Then he drew her against him so completely that she could feel the long hard lines of him.

He was already aroused, she realised wonderingly, his body vibrantly alive. She'd had this effect on him?

She had planned to resist, but instead she wound her arms about his neck. She couldn't help it. And he deepened the kiss, went on kissing her for a long, long time, and when their lips finally parted Jodi was trembling all over, speechless. All she could say was, 'Oh...Griff...'

He held her a little away from him, his eyes searching her face. 'All right?' he asked. He sounded genuinely concerned.

'Yes, but... I really think——'

'Don't think,' he suggested gently. 'Just let yourself feel. If you let yourself think too much your mind will protest, as always. Let your natural instincts guide you instead.'

He renewed his kisses, and now his hands began to move over the smooth skin of her neck and shoulders, his lips following the same path. Jodi sighed softly and went unresistingly when he pulled her close once more.

His kisses, his caresses were drugging her, casting a spell of enchantment, of lethargy. There was no more resistance in her. She buried her hands in his thick dark hair, her fingers moving convulsively. She pressed herself against him, wanting to get closer—and closer still.

Her reactions seemed to awake an even stronger response in him, for the touch of his hands became fiercer, more possessive. He pulled the lower half of her body more firmly against his own, making her all too aware of his need, a need that was growing within her too.

But when his fingers invaded the neckline of her dress, seeking her breasts, she realised dimly that it was time to call a halt.

With a strength she wouldn't have believed possible a few moments ago, she pushed him away. 'No, Griff,' she said firmly. 'That's far enough.' A swift glance at the mantel clock reinforced her next words. 'And you've had your half-hour.'

'And you intend to keep me strictly to my ration?' He sounded angry. Dammit, he had no right to be angry. He'd brought her here—insisted on staying, forced his attentions...

No, be fair, she told herself; he hadn't forced her. Persuaded her, yes—and perhaps she hadn't needed that much persuading. But she had never intended that things should get out of hand.

'That was the agreement,' she said evenly. She stood up, smoothing down her hair, her dress. 'Besides, it's late. Two o'clock in the morning—Monday morning. I assume you have to work today?'

'As it happens, no.' His tone was cold, but his breathing was still slightly ragged. 'One of the advantages of being management. But you've made your point. I'll take you home.'

He need not sound so aggrieved, Jodi thought indignantly as he closed up the house and fetched their coats. On the whole she thought she had treated his high-handed behaviour with more tolerance than it deserved.

'Good night last night?' Sally wanted to know.

'Mmm, so-so.' For once, Jodi did not feel like giving her sister a detailed account. She was tired after her late night. But it wasn't that. In the past she'd had no compunction about retailing, in humorous fashion, the abortive attempts of her dates to get past her defences. Somehow she didn't want to discuss Griff and what had occurred between them. She changed the subject. 'How are you? You look a bit peaky this morning.'

'I don't feel too good,' Sally admitted. 'Touch of flu, perhaps. My stomach feels a bit gripey.'

'Why don't you go back to bed? I can take Tanya with me when I run Robin to nursery.'

'Thanks,' Sally said gratefully. 'I'll take you up on that.'

Washing, dressing and feeding two small children, getting Robin to nursery on time, needed single-minded concentration. And during that time Jodi was able to put last night to the back of her mind.

But later, in the silent house, with Sally sleeping upstairs, there was too much opportunity for thought.

Griff had been very quiet on the way back. He'd escorted her up the slippery path to Sally's door, but he had made no attempt at a farewell kiss. Contrarily, she'd wished he would. It seemed wrong to part like this after what had happened earlier. It was too abrupt, as though a life-support system had suddenly, brutally been switched off.

But that was the way you wanted it, she reminded herself. The analogy that had sprung to mind, 'life-support system', was an alarming one—as though his lovemaking had become essential to her well-being. Which it wasn't, she told herself firmly.

Which made it all the more annoying that she should feel so depressed all day. She was willing to bet Griff wasn't brooding around the place. She doubted somehow that he had been entirely celibate since his wife's death. There was nothing about him that proclaimed the ascetic. There were probably other women he dated, rivals for his affection.

Rivals? Why had that word occurred to her, for heaven's sake? She wasn't competing for him. She was trying to give him the brush-off—wasn't she?

Wednesday morning's post brought her a slim package. Busy with the children, for Sally was still feeling off colour, Jodi had no time to open it immediately. But in any case it wasn't from Griff, she reassured herself. The direction label was typed, not handwritten.

It was coffee-time before she had leisure to examine the package. She ripped it open, then stared uncomprehendingly at the contents.

At first she thought it was the genuine article, something she had only seen in museums. But closer inspection proved it to be a clever mock-up of a wartime ration book.

Already warning bells were beginning to ring as she opened the cover to find—not coupons for food and clothing. Instead, each little square was inscribed with varying portions of time—ten minutes, half an hour,

an hour. One of the half-hour coupons had been
clipped out.

A further search of the wrappings revealed a note
she had missed at first glance. In Griff's bold hand-
writing it said:

> If you're reading this my ruse has worked.
> Knowing you, anything in my handwriting would
> have been binned.

Oh, he knew her all right. He was altogether too
perceptive for her liking. She read on, and was torn
between indignation and unwilling amusement.

> You'll see that Sunday night's ration has been
> accounted for. By my reckoning I'm now owed two
> days. I'll be round to collect.

But when? If only she knew that, she could arrange
to be out, let him see she had no intention of dancing
attendance on his whims. But she couldn't stay out
indefinitely. She was here to keep Sally company.

She could refuse to answer the door, she supposed.
But, knowing Griff, that would achieve nothing. He
was quite capable of standing on the doorstep, at-
tracting the unwelcome attention of the neighbours.
This was a respectable neighbourhood, and Sally and
Barry had to go on living here, even if she didn't.

Oh, let him come. As well try to stop the tide as
prevent Griff from doing something his mind was set
on.

It was something of a shock to Jodi to catch herself
smiling at the thought of his persistence, to realise
that she had been smiling rather a lot recently. And
now that she tried to analyse just why everything had
seemed so much fun of late she was dismayed to find

that it was all down to Griff, that he was assuming far too much importance in her life.

For some reason she had assumed that he would not be too far behind his letter, and when there was no sign of him that evening she felt unreasonably let down. By Thursday afternoon he had still not contacted her.

'You're getting withdrawal symptoms,' Sally teased, and for once Jodi was not quite so swift with her denials. Uneasily, she reflected that her sister might very well be right.

Instead, she said, 'It's the twenty-third today. I don't suppose I'll see him again now until after Christmas. It is a family time, after all.'

How soon, she wondered, before Griff could reasonably be expected to be free of family commitments? Perhaps not until the New Year. There was his business to be taken into consideration too. Christmas and New Year were busy times for big department stores.

Realising the trend her thoughts were taking, she jerked herself up sharply. What have you got to feel so low about? she asked herself. If you were Sally you'd have a reason to feel sorry for yourself.

Thinking of Sally and the children reminded her that she had not yet wrapped up all their presents and she was out of decorative paper.

'I just have to slip down to the newsagents,' she told her sister. And to Robin, 'Want to come for a walk?'

'Are we buying sweeties?' he asked hopefully.

'I dare say,' with a rueful grin at Sally's despairing shake of the head.

Choosing her wrapping paper took her half the time that it took Robin to choose his sweets, and when she got back to the house she found her sister eagerly awaiting her.

'Griff phoned. He said...' and Sally looked puzzled '...I think I got the message right—to have your ration book ready for tonight. Do you know what he means?'

'Oh, yes, I know,' Jodi said, aware of a ridiculous smile that felt as if it were stretched from ear to ear.

'If I didn't know differently,' Sally said, 'I'd say you were extremely pleased at the thought of seeing Griff tonight.'

She was. She couldn't deny it. As she studied the contents of her wardrobe that evening, Jodi knew she had given up fighting the situation. From the first moment she and Griff had met, control of her life seemed to have slipped from her grasp, and she found she no longer resented it.

After trying on and discarding several dresses, she finally decided on one she had not yet worn. The particular shade of blue was very flattering to her silvery fair hair and the colour subtly changed her grey eyes to a warmer hue.

'Wow!' Sally exclaimed, seeing her ready long before the expected hour of eight. 'If he wasn't already totally besotted he'd have no chance tonight.'

Jodi laughed. But for once she did not feel compelled to scorn her sister's prediction. 'You're sure you don't mind being stuck with Griff's secretary again?' she asked.

'Of course not. I like her. I'm even thinking of asking her to visit us over Christmas. What do you think? It can't be much fun being alone at holiday time.'

Sitting beside Griff as he drove, Jodi couldn't help wondering how the evening would turn out. He hadn't said where he was taking her. All she knew was that they were going for a meal. But what would follow that she had no idea.

Her insides shook at the possibility that he might take her somewhere again, where he could make love to her. And she knew that this time she would not protest.

The restaurant Griff had selected followed the usual pattern, in that it was totally unlike anywhere else they had been. But given Griff's taste for good food and good wine, she guessed the cuisine would be of a high standard.

Again he had booked a secluded alcove, where they could see but not be seen—or heard—by the other diners, some of whom she recognised as acquaintances.

The waiter would have seated her, but Griff insisted on doing so himself, taking the opportunity to breathe in her ear, 'I hope you brought your ration book?'

She had, although she'd felt rather silly doing so. She produced it from her handbag.

'May I?' He reached across the table, then without even looking at the book slipped it into his breast pocket.

'Why did you do that?' she asked. She had expected him to carry on the joke, apportion some of her time to himself.

'Because I've decided that—from now on—*all* your time belongs to me.'

She gasped. Earlier in their acquaintance it might have been a gasp of outrage. Now it was a shocked reaction to her own sensations. He sounded so purposeful, so... so sure.

'The jokes are over, Jodi,' he went on. 'From now on this is serious—deadly serious.' His gaze was caressive. It was almost as if he were physically tracing the outlines of her body. It made her feel—vulnerable.

'I...I see.' As a comment it was a pretty feeble one. But she couldn't think of anything else to say. What had happened to all the smart deflating remarks she'd used in the past to quell other men's pretensions? Suddenly she knew why they had escaped her. She didn't need them. She didn't want to deflect Griff's attention.

She smiled at him, an uninhibited curving of her generous mouth, and saw his eyes widen, their colour deepen.

'Jodi?' He reached across the table once more, but this time to take her hand. 'Jodi, I——'

'Here's the menu, sir.'

The outstretched hand was snatched back and she saw rather than heard him curse as he accepted the leatherbound book from the man's hand.

The matter of the meal disposed of, there was their wine to order. Despite her increasing eagerness for his company and—yes, she had to be honest with herself at least—his lovemaking, Jodi wasn't sorry for this respite. Things were moving a little too fast tonight. She must not let him fluster her.

While Griff dealt with the wine she allowed her gaze to travel round the room, noting with some satisfaction that there wasn't another man there who could touch Griff for looks or sheer compelling presence.

A couple just entering the restaurant attracted her attention, and she gave a little gasp of dismay. Rodney! Their paths hadn't crossed since their bitter, acrimonious parting. What was he doing here?

Then she realised how ridiculous that was. There was, after all, just as much likelihood of his visiting this restaurant as there was of her doing so. But what an awful coincidence that they should both be here at the same time.

But seeing him was a reminder of the reason for all her defensive barriers—barriers which Griff had managed to infiltrate, barriers she had been considering removing entirely.

'What is it?' Griff had heard her involuntary exclamation, and now his eyes followed hers to where the couple were just seating themselves at their table. His eyes narrowed. 'Who's that?' he demanded.

'J-just someone I know.'

'Boyfriend?'

'Ex-boyfriend, but... Oh, Griff...' She half rose. 'I'm... I'm sorry, but we have to go. I can't——'

'You don't want him to see you with me?' Griff's eyes had hardened dangerously.

'No, it's not that. I——'

'Jodi!' He sounded exasperated now. 'Pull yourself together. What exactly is all this about—if you're not afraid to be seen with me? We can't leave—our meal's been ordered. We——'

'Please!' she begged him. But at the same time she rose from her seat. With or without Griff, she was leaving. The sight of Rodney had completely ruined the evening for her.

'Oh, very well.' But Griff looked absolutely furious as he came round the table.

Even so, she was glad of his firm supporting grasp of her elbow as he steered her between the tables, stopping briefly to acquaint the waiter of their departure. She heard him offer an apology and some excuse, but her mind was not on his words. She wanted to get out of here before Rodney noticed her.

Too late.

'Jodi, by all that's wonderful! Long time no see!' He had risen and was advancing towards her, hands outstretched, for all the world, she thought indignantly, as though he expected an equally warm greeting from her. 'I've been meaning to get in touch. Lucille and I aren't together any more, and I——'

'Then who's that?' she demanded tautly, jerking her head towards his dinner companion.

'Oh...' Rodney waved a negligent hand '...just business. One of the buyers from——'

'Just as I was only business,' she muttered, remembering how close she had come to going into partnership with him.

The old anger and distaste for this man, the remembrance of betrayal, was rising up in her, making her totally oblivious to her surroundings. It was Griff's voice that recalled her, blessedly restoring her presence of mind, a sense of proportion.

'Excuse me!' His tone was clipped, still edged with the anger he had shown at the table. 'My fiancée and I are in a hurry.'

'He's your fiancé?' Rodney looked at Jodi for confirmation.

Still startled herself by Griff's words, she had no chance to decide how to answer. Griff was hurrying her on, sidestepping Rodney. But by the time he settled her in the car she was feeling hideously embarrassed and not a little annoyed with him for his public announcement. Several people nearby must have heard him—people who knew her.

'Why on earth did you say that?' she demanded crossly, as he slid into the driving seat.

'You looked in need of moral support.'

'I was—but not to that extent.' Then she remembered that he had forgone his meal on her account. 'But thanks for the thought—and I'm sorry.'

'Sorry for what?' He still sounded grim.

'For making you miss dinner.'

He would probably take her home now, and the evening for which—she couldn't deny it—she'd prepared with such anticipation would be ruined—was already ruined. She wondered uneasily if fate had decided on that encounter as a warning to her not to relax her guard where men were concerned. If so, the warning had come a little late. But perhaps not too late. Perhaps it would be as well if Griff did take her home.

But instead he drove up on to the Heath, parked and switched on the interior light, then turned to look at her.

'And now I'd like an explanation. Just what does that bumptious fool mean to you?'

Bumptious? she thought wonderingly. Now why had she never seen Rodney in that light? The description fitted him so aptly, made him ludicrous, destroying much of his sinister image in her eyes.

'Well?' Griff repeated. 'Why were you so anxious to avoid him?'

'He . . . I——'

'You said he was an ex-boyfriend?' His tone was sharp, almost as if . . . as if he was jealous. She couldn't help the feeling of warmth that spread through her at the thought. 'Is he still "ex" as far as you're concerned?' And as she nodded, 'So why did we have to leave? Why were you so frightened of facing him?' And before she could say anything, 'Do you imagine you're still in love with him? Is that it?'

'No, I do not!' she said indignantly. 'Oh, I thought I was once, until I found him out. Seeing him again reminded me... Well, anyway, I just didn't want to be in the same room as the cheating, conniving——'

'He cheated on you—with another woman?' Griff sounded incredulous. 'The man must be even more of a fool than I took him for.'

Jodi's subconscious recognised the compliment, but Rodney had also been adept at flattery, she thought darkly—and deception.

'More than that,' she told Griff. 'He came close to cheating my partner and me out of our business too. We were within a hair's breadth of joining forces with him. It only needed our signatures on a couple of documents.'

'You found him out in time?'

'Yes, thank goodness—about his business swindles and the fact that he was two-timing me.'

'I'm surprised he's not in prison, if he's a swindler.'

'He came close. But he got off on some technicality. He got a heavy fine instead. So he's free to go round conning other unsuspecting women,' she concluded bitterly.

'I presume it was your boutique that was endangered?'

'Yes—and now it seems to be at risk again.' And she found herself telling him about Lucinda's defection and about the possibility of losing the premises altogether.

'I had a lucky escape with Rodney, but now I look like falling into someone else's clutches. It's not funny,' she snapped as a smile flickered across his face.

'I'm sorry. I wasn't laughing at your business problems—just your turn of phrase.' His manner altered suddenly and he set a hand on hers. 'I've been hoping,' he said huskily, 'that it's my clutches you'll be falling into. Jodi, we get on so well together, but there's something missing. You know what it is as well as I do.'

Sudden panic made her pulses flutter. 'No,' she denied quickly.

'Yes, you do. We haven't made love yet. Jodi,' throatily, 'we need to get to know each other better— much, much better.'

With the resurrected past so recently before her, his words made Jodi flinch. 'No, Griff... I'm not going to——'

'Aren't you?' he said softly. 'I think I might be able to change your mind about that.'

Suddenly he was out of his seatbelt, had her free of hers. And then she was in his arms, his mouth covering hers, fiercely possessive. 'I,' he told her confidently, 'am going to drive out any and every thought you might have about any other man.'

At first she struggled against him, tried to resist, still convinced that meeting Rodney tonight had been a warning. But gradually his ardent kisses, his caresses began to exert their irresistible spell.

This was different from all her former encounters, she excused her growing weakness. This time it was not just the man himself she was fighting but herself, her own reactions to him.

'Jodi,' Griff muttered throatily, 'relax—it's time you stopped being afraid of your own sensuality, time you learned to live dangerously, to discover what you've been missing.'

Two against one was unfair, especially when one was your own traitorous body. Jodi gave up the unequal struggle, threw away all her self-imposed rules. Griff was right. Despite all her attempts to maintain the contrary, until now something had been lacking in her life, and she didn't want to wait any longer to belong to someone—really belong. As she responded to his kiss a groan escaped him.

The touch of his lips on hers became increasingly sensual, his tongue probing her lips, making her blood burn molten fire in her veins. Her head was swimming and—completely lost to sanity—she plunged feverish hands into his thick hair, her mouth moving under his, little cries of need escaping her.

Griff lifted his head just long enough to say, 'I want you, Jodi. I've wanted you from the very first moment I saw you. Forget that cretin we saw tonight. Don't waste your emotions on him. He would never have been right for you.'

Her heart beating an irregular tattoo, Jodi acknowledged to herself that she wanted him too. She wanted him to make love to her. And he was wrong. She couldn't care less about Rodney. She was in love— and her heart did a giddy somersault—she was in love with Griff, had been for some while, only she had been afraid to admit it.

This discovery threw her so much that she was incapable of resistance when she felt his hand unbutton her coat and then slide inside the V-neck of her dress. His touch was warm, seeking, and when his hand cupped one swollen breast, his thumb caressing its hardened peak, she cried out in a mingling of delight and anguish.

'I want you, Jodi,' he said again. 'And you want me too, don't you?'

'Yes,' she admitted huskily.

He groaned again. 'Oh God, I need you so much, but I can't make proper love to you here.' He held her a little away from him and looked deeply into her eyes. 'Promise me, Jodi, if I stop kissing you long enough to drive us somewhere else, you won't go cold on me.'

Too full of emotion to say much, she nodded. 'I promise.'

'Your friend's still away?' she asked as the car pulled up in Hampstead village.

'Until the New Year,' Griff confirmed.

They hadn't exchanged a single word on the way here, but Griff had driven with one hand resting on her knee, a hand that had occasionally moved up to caress her thigh, his touch flooding her body with heat, increasing her pitch of feverish desire.

He didn't pause in the living area this time, but instead swept her up into his arms and carried her up the narrow staircase.

'This is the room I use when I stay here,' he said as he gathered her into his arms.

His kiss was tender at first, but there was no way he could sustain such gentleness for long. His body throbbed against hers, the kiss deepened in intimacy, and with it their mutual need.

'I'm sorry, Jodi,' he muttered huskily against her throat, 'I'd meant to make love to you slowly, until you needed me as much as I need you, but I... Oh, God...' His voice trailed off into incoherence.

Somehow, without releasing her, he managed to remove her dress, her bra and panties following it to the floor. Kissing her, caressing her, he coaxed her towards the bed. But she needed no persuading. All she knew was that she loved Griff and that nothing else mattered but that he should make love to her— here—now.

'Oh, Griff,' she breathed as he moved with her on to the bed, trailing kisses down over her throat, her breasts, his fingers doing magical things to the rest of her body. 'Oh, Griff!' And this time she cried his name aloud as her need became unbearable.

He moved to enter her, and pleasure was diminished for an instant by sudden pain.

Griff went very still. 'Dear God,' he muttered. 'Why didn't you tell me you were still a virgin? I thought...'

'No,' she said fiercely, 'Rodney and I never... Does... does it matter so much?' she asked. 'Oh, please, Griff...' She clung to him, afraid that he would move away.

'It doesn't matter,' he confirmed huskily. 'My God, of course it doesn't matter. I just feel very privileged to be the first... I really had no idea...'

With gentle consideration, he completed his penetration, paused until he felt her relax, then slowly he began to move again. But such iron control was impossible to maintain for long, and she clung to him frantically as shuddering paroxysms seized his body and at the very height of his climax he cried her name aloud, burying his face against her breasts.

After a moment or two he lifted his head and kissed her softly. 'I'm sorry,' he groaned, 'I'd meant to wait—to take you with me. I promise you, it won't always be like that.'

'It's ... it's all right.' But she lied—for every nerve, every cheated sense screamed out for fulfilment.

But he knew that she lied, and now with hands and mouth he began a slow sensual foray upon her body until at last, with a little sob of joy, she too found release.

She must have dozed for some while afterwards, and for a moment she couldn't think where she was, until her eyes focused on a bare masculine chest.

Now reaction set in and dismay flooded through her. What had she done? For the first time in her life she had allowed her heart to rule her head, or—on a cynical note—her body to overrule common sense. But she was not given time to brood or dwell on the panic that threatened to overwhelm her.

'Welcome back,' Griff murmured. His arm came around her, pulling her naked body close to his once more. 'I've been watching you,' he told her huskily, 'and it took all my self-control to let you have your sleep out.'

He was making up for that self-denial now, as he began to caress her once more, his eyes on her face watching the re-arousal of a desire she could not hide.

It was going to be all right, she told herself as fear evaporated and logical thought began to blur and evade her once again. Griff was different. He would never hurt her. There would be no deceit, no betrayal. Once more she gave herself up to rapture.

* * *

'You might have let me know you planned to stay out all night,' Sally said. Her complaint was half serious, half humorous. But her sister looked pale and drawn this morning, Jodi noticed. 'In the end—in sheer self-preservation—I just had to offer Mrs Monkton a bed. Neither of us could keep our eyes open any longer.'

'I'm sorry, Sal.' Jodi was penitent. 'But I didn't plan to stay out. It . . . it just happened.'

But was that quite true? So far as she was concerned it had been, but what about Griff?

After they had made love for the second time, she'd told him she must go home.

'I can't leave Sally and the children all night,' she'd explained.

But Griff, pulling her close once more, had refused to stir. 'Mrs M is quite prepared to stay over if need be.'

And the closeness of him, the things he was doing to her, had prevented her from examining that statement too closely. But now, in the light of day, without his disruptive presence to cloud her thoughts, she wondered. Had he warned his secretary that he intended to be gone all night? Had he really been so sure of her? Despite her ready capitulation, she found she didn't like that idea, didn't like it at all.

She might have abandoned her own resolve, but she would have preferred to think of it as something that had happened spontaneously without premeditation—to both of them.

'I really am sorry, Sal,' she said again. And, 'You don't look too good. Why not go back to bed?'

Sally shook her head. 'I can't seem to get comfortable lately. I had some quite bad pains in the night.'

'Labour pains? And I wasn't here!' Guilt flooded Jodi. She was supposed to be looking after her sister, and instead she had been indulging in self-gratification. 'Why didn't you get Mrs Monkton to phone the doctor?'

'It doesn't feel like labour pains.' Sally grimaced suddenly, her hand moving to her abdomen.

'You've still got it.' Jodi jumped up. 'I'm calling the doctor right now.'

'No, don't fuss. It's probably just the baby pressing on a nerve.'

But Jodi was adamant. 'Better safe than sorry.'

After that things seemed to move very rapidly. The doctor was there within minutes, and within half an hour of Jodi's phone call, her sister was on her way to hospital.

'Almost certainly appendicitis,' the doctor had said. 'What a time to get it!'

Christmas Eve, and Jodi was left with the festivities in ruins about her. Tanya was too young to understand, but what sort of Christmas would it be for Robin, with both parents absent?

Added to that consideration was her anxiety for Sally and the unborn baby. Especially since the doctor had agreed that she ought to try and contact Barry. Things must be serious for him to say that.

Suddenly Jodi felt very alone and frightened. For perhaps the first time in her life she was realising that self-sufficiency was cold comfort. Griff's words came back to her. 'Independence may be all very well when you're young—but what about when you're older? Or when things go wrong? You could be very lonely.'

If only Griff were here now. Not to help her look after the children. She could cope with them. But she needed someone to talk to—about her concern, her fears for Sally. Suppose Sally were to…to die? Nausea swept through her and she felt tears begin to well up.

Pull yourself together, she admonished herself sternly. It's not going to help Sally or the children if you go to pieces. This is no time for self-indulgence. Your first job is to get on that phone to Barry's emergency number.

Even so, her fingers shook as she dialled. She had not expected to be able to speak to Barry himself, and such was the case. Her message was taken by an impersonal voice, and when she put the receiver down it was still with no idea when her brother-in-law would be able to contact her.

Moving like an automaton, she gave Robin and Tanya their lunch. Soon after the little girl was taking a nap, but there was still Robin to amuse. Jodi had never felt less playful. If only there had been nursery today, but all facilities had closed down for the holiday.

The need to talk to someone was growing by the minute. Griff was the logical person, but he had been going into the store today. Traditionally Christmas Eve was a mad last-minute rush and his hand would be needed at the helm.

Then she thought of Mrs Monkton. She was not working today, Griff had said when Jodi had worried about keeping his secretary up so late. 'She's got the day off. There's never time on Christmas Eve for routine paperwork.'

Mrs Monkton had given Sally her telephone number. Jodi leafed through her sister's personal directory.

To her relief there was an immediate reply to her call, and soon she was pouring out the story to sympathetic ears.

'I'll come round straight away,' Mrs Monkton said at the conclusion of her narrative. 'You'll want to go to the hospital. I'll look after the children.'

She still had to exercise patience. Mrs Monkton lived an hour's drive away. But even so Jodi was ready with her coat on when the doorbell rang. She hurried to answer it.

But as she opened the door, she was caught up in strong arms, held tightly against a broad chest.

'My poor love. I came as soon as I heard.'

'Oh, Griff!' Her voice wobbled treacherously as she clung gladly, unquestioningly to him. 'I'm so glad you're here!'

'I'll always be here for you, Jodi,' he promised. 'Always.'

CHAPTER FIVE

JODI hadn't questioned Griff's miraculous arrival, but he explained anyway.

'Mrs Monkton called me—I was nearer, and she thought I'd want to know about Sally. Try not to worry, Jodi. As soon as Mrs M arrives I'm taking you to the hospital.'

Relief flooded her, but she felt bound to demur, 'But you must be so busy——'

'Jodi, one of the arts of management—as you yourself obviously know, since you've left your assistants in charge of your boutique—is delegation. I admit I like being in the thick of things myself, especially at Christmas, supplying the personal touch, but this is more important—far more important. Sally's welfare is more important. And you,' he stressed, 'are more important—to me.'

'I telephoned the hospital while I was waiting for Mrs Monkton,' Jodi told him as they drove away. 'But at that stage they couldn't tell me anything. Perhaps I'll be able to see someone—a doctor——?'

'We'll stay there until there's news,' Griff reassured her.

'This is good of you,' Jodi told him as they took a seat in a small side-room with the prospect of a long wait ahead of them. 'I feel terribly guilty, taking up so much of your time. Waiting for news is just agony for me—I'm so scared. But for you it must be plain boring.'

'Nonsense,' Griff said firmly, 'I share your concern—I'm very fond of Sally. Besides, I could never be bored when I'm with you—and I intend to be with you a lot more in future. Jodi, we have a lot to discuss—where we're going to live, for example, and how soon. I warn you, I'm not prepared to wait long. I want you all to myself, and very soon.'

'Oh!' Jodi gasped. As yet she hadn't thought beyond her newly discovered love for Griff. For now that had been enough. And any permanent commitment deserved serious thought—since, for her, it would have to be forever. She could never settle for anything less, and she had to be certain he shared that belief. His marriage had been a happy one, and for all his claims that he had recovered from the sorrow of his loss, he might be—albeit subconsciously—reluctant to risk another permanent relationship.

So far he certainly hadn't actually mentioned marriage, even though... 'I know you told Rodney... But I thought that was just——' she began.

'I know I haven't actually asked you to marry me, but——'

'Griff!' Hastily, before he could go on and perhaps ruin everything, she interrupted, 'Please, don't say any more right now. You see, I'm not sure yet that...'

His lips tightened. 'Are you trying to tell me last night meant nothing at all to you?' Scornfully, 'I didn't think you were the kind of girl who——'

'I'm not—it did,' she said incoherently. 'But I must be honest—it...it just happened. I didn't intend that it should happen. I——'

'I see,' he interrupted before she could explain further. 'It seems I've been presuming too much.'

He was grim now, withdrawn from her into some inner fastness where she could not reach him. He was with her physically, but mentally, spiritually she was alone again. She couldn't bear it.

'Oh, please, Griff, don't look like that. Don't take it this way. We should never have started discussing something like this now. I can't think straight—not with Sally...' Jodi choked on her sister's name and jumped up to stare blindly out of the window.

'Jodi!' He was behind her in an instant, his hands on her shoulders, turning her into his arms. 'I'm sorry—that was damned selfish of me. You're right, this isn't the time or the place to try and sort out our future.' He put a hand under her chin and tilted up her face so that he could see it, her great grey eyes glazed with tears, the quivering lips. 'It's all right, my dear, I won't pressure you any more. It shall be just how you want it. All I ask is that you don't cast me out of your life altogether—hmm?'

'I...I won't do that,' she promised shakily. 'It's me who's being selfish now, Griff. I...I can't commit myself to...to anything just now. But I do need you here with me.'

'I'll settle for that—for now.' He pulled her close again, and somehow she felt imbued with his strength. 'Take heart, my love. I'm sure all will be well with Sally. She's in good hands, and where medicine is concerned, we're not living in the Dark Ages now!'

Nevertheless the hours that followed were among the most trying in Jodi's life. For the most part they sat quietly, her cold hand in Griff's strong warm one.

When they spoke at all it was mostly of Sally, of the children, of the likelihood of Barry getting home.

'Suppose . . . suppose he's too late?' Jodi couldn't help saying at one point. 'How could I face him—tell him?' And then out poured the guilt which had been building up ever since that morning. 'If only I'd been home last night——'

'Now stop that!' Griff was gently stern with her. 'Even if you had been at home, your sister might not have woken you, any more than she woke Mrs Monkton.'

'We can't know that. I'm family, I should have been there.'

'If you're so set on blaming yourself,' he said quietly, 'I suppose you must blame me too?'

She looked at him, but she couldn't deny it. In her anxiety, her thoughts had been tending that way. If only he'd taken her home when she'd asked him.

'I see you do blame me,' he said quietly.

'I . . . I can't help it.'

What he might have said then she was not to discover. For at that moment a nurse appeared to tell Jodi that the doctor would see her now.

Heart thudding, stomach churning, she leapt to her feet. Griff rose with her, a steadying hand on her arm.

'Are you a relation?' the nurse asked Griff, patently implying that, if he were not, he must remain where he was.

The doctor's relaxed manner, his smile, calmed Jodi's worst fears. He confirmed that Sally's agonising pains had been due to a badly inflamed appendix. And in view of the seriousness of her condition it had been decided to carry out an immediate Caesarean, followed by an appendectomy while she was still under the anaesthetic.

'This entailed two teams of surgeons working one after the other,' he explained.

'No wonder it took so long,' Jodi said. 'But is she——?'

'She's fine,' the doctor reassured her. 'She's asleep now, so I'm afraid you can't see her. And obviously she'll have to stay in hospital a lot longer than if things had been normal. By the way,' he added, 'you might like to know—the baby was a boy.'

When Jodi returned to the little waiting-room, tears were streaming down her face. Relief had achieved something that anxiety had not, breaking down her dammed-up emotions.

Griff took one look at her, then strode towards her, his own features contorted.

'Jodi? My God! Sally's not——? She hasn't——?'

'No,' she managed to gulp as his arms went round her. 'She's all right. I'm sorry—it's just such a relief.'

'Thank God! Thank God!' He hugged her tightly. 'And don't apologise. Cry all you want. You've been so brave—it wasn't natural. I was beginning to worry about you.'

As she clung to him, revelling in the comfort of his arms, Jodi knew just how desperately she did want to share the rest of her life with this man—on any terms. After all, these days many relationships were as permanent as marriage. As in marriage, there would be moments of ecstasy—and as with all lives there would be troubles and anxieties. But she could face those as long as she and Griff were together. And she had told him she wasn't sure.

For a moment she was tempted to tell him she had changed her mind, but she felt uncomfortable at the idea of doing so. It didn't seem the right time, the right mood. Surely there would be another, more suitable occasion? And besides, if he really loved her he would raise the subject again himself. As she had long since discovered, Griff was nothing if not persistent.

'It's not going to be much of a Christmas for Robin and Tanya,' Griff commented as he drove her home. 'Sally in hospital, their father abroad.'

Jodi had to agree. 'And even if Barry does fly home, once he knows Sally's OK, he'll probably have to go straight back again.'

'It won't be much fun for you either,' he suggested. 'All alone in that house, except for two small children.'

Secretly Jodi had been thinking the same, but she hadn't much choice. She shrugged. 'Oh, I'm used to being on my own. I've always preferred living alone.'

'Oh?' It was swiftly asked, and there was an odd note in his voice. Jodi looked at him sharply, realising what he was thinking.

'I meant I don't normally live with Sally and I've never shared with anyone. I prefer to be independent.'

Grimly, 'So I've noticed.'

He was silent for a while, and then, as they neared the house, he said, 'You must come to us.'

'Us?' She had half expected but then discounted the possibility of an invitation to spend the holiday with him, and the thought had crossed her mind that, with the children, they would have been just like a family.

'I'm spending Christmas with my parents,' he explained.

'Oh, no,' Jodi shook her head. 'Christmas is a family time. I wouldn't dream of imposing——'

'It wouldn't be any imposition. They have an enormous house, and it's going to be very empty this year. I'm the only one going home.'

She waited for him to say he particularly wanted her to meet his parents. Instead he said, 'Mum and Dad will be missing all the grandchildren this year. They'd love to have Robin and Tanya to fuss over.'

He was obviously more concerned about the children's Christmas and his parents' pleasure than hers. Oh, well, she had only herself to blame for that, and—with a sense of shame—Christmas was more for children, after all. Even so, she felt obscurely depressed.

He ushered her into the house, and the next few moments were spent in assuring Mrs Monkton that Sally and her baby were both doing well. Jodi explained to Robin that he now had a small brother, 'Even smaller than Tanya,' she told him.

'Right!' Griff said briskly. 'Pack up what you need for yourself and the children. I'll get on the phone to my mother and tell her to expect us.'

'But if she's not expecting many people this year... What about food? She won't have——'

'Don't worry!' He swept this objection aside. 'My mother always caters as if for an army. You'll be doing me and Dad a favour—we're the ones who always have to finish up any leftovers.'

'And then there's Mrs Monkton,' Jodi lowered her voice. 'Sally had invited her——'

'All taken care of. Mrs M comes too.'

'I don't even know where your parents live. Is it far? What about visiting Sally?'

'They're not far from London, so I'll drive you in each day. Any more problems?' he asked ironically. 'Or is it me you object to spending Christmas with?'

'No, of course not.' Spending Christmas with him would be marvellous, and a chance to see him in domestic circumstances. Most people had two images—a public and a private one. It could be very enlightening to spend time with Griff on his home ground.

Not knowing his parents, she had felt bound to demur. It was not something you did lightly, intruding upon a family gathering, particularly at Christmas. Now, all her reservations brushed aside in Griff's usual determined manner, she yielded gratefully.

Half an hour later they were on their way, stopping only en route at Jodi's flat to check on her mail, something she'd not had time to do since she'd been at Sally's. Most of it was Christmas mail, she decided, but there were one or two official-looking envelopes, bills, bank statements and so on. These she thrust into her handbag to be dealt with at her leisure.

The journey was occupied by explaining to Robin that because Mummy was poorly, they would be spending Christmas with Uncle Griff's mummy and daddy. Robin was highly diverted to discover that grown-ups had mummies and daddies too.

'But how will Father Christmas know where to bring my presents if I'm not at my home?' he asked anxiously.

Jodi smiled, thinking of a certain suitcase in the boot totally devoted to gaily wrapped parcels, and she was able to reassure him with complete certainty that,

'Father Christmas is very clever. He'll find you all right.'

Griff had described his parents' home as being large, a vague description which had left Jodi very little wiser. The actuality left her totally stunned.

Two hours out of London into the Kentish countryside, a sudden turn in a quiet lane brought an enormous Tudor-style house into view. The black beams against the white countryside were an impressive sight, and Jodi exclaimed with delight.

'What a beautiful old place! Is it a stately home? National Trust property?'

She heard Mrs Monkton chuckle, and Griff too seemed amused.

'Thank goodness, no,' he said. 'That's my parents' place.'

'That's your home?' For a moment Jodi stared at him in shocked disbelief. But this was not one of his jokes, she realised, and she knew a sudden sense of uneasy foreboding.

Set well back at the end of a long drive fringed by tall trees, the house was fronted by parkland, grazed in spring, Griff told her, by deer. 'My father keeps a small model herd. In winter they're brought into byres at the rear of the house.'

Jodi stared ahead. The nearer they came to the house the more impressive it all looked and the lower her spirits sank. She had known, of course, that Griff and his family couldn't be exactly poverty-stricken; Griffiths Brothers was a large, prestigious company with branches in other major cities. But his family were obviously also considerable landowners—and Griff was their eldest son, presumably the heir to all this.

And she had been thinking that the Christmas holiday might provide her with a suitable occasion during which to lead up to the subject of his suggestion that they live together—to let it be known, delicately, that a repetition of that suggestion would be welcome.

But now.... Now it would look as if she had been influenced by this discovery of the extent of his wealth. She had no wish to appear in his eyes as a calculating gold-digger. Even if he were to renew his suggestion, without any prompting, it would be bound to occur to him afterwards that she had only accepted upon seeing his family home.

And what of his family? Almost certainly his parents would want their eldest son to remarry, to give them grandchildren, future heirs to all this grandeur.

Jodi sighed. It seemed there was no end to the problems besetting their relationship. And yet she couldn't wish that she had never met Griff.

Then, suddenly, there was no more time for brooding as she was caught up in the bustle of arrival. Unlike his aunt, Robin was not at all daunted by his surroundings. Released from his seatbelt, he was out of the car and running towards the broad front steps, at the head of which a heavy oak door had swung hospitably open. Someone had been watching out for their arrival.

Framed in the doorway were—not servants as Jodi had begun to expect, but a well-dressed couple who were unmistakably Griff's parents. From his father he had inherited his height and muscular bulk, from his mother his colouring and facial characteristics, though Griff's were set in a stronger mould.

Tanya in her arms, Griff's hand at her elbow, Jodi found herself mounting the steps, uncomfortably aware that she was still wearing the jeans and sweater in which she had made her dash to the hospital and that it was some days since she'd had her last regular hairdressing appointment. Whatever would this well-groomed couple think of her?

At least there was no doubt about the warmth of their welcome. Although, as Mrs Griffiths scooped Tanya from Jodi's arms, cooing enthusiastically at the chubby mite, and Mr Griffiths swung Robin up on to his broad shoulder, Jodi did rather wonder for whom the welcome was intended.

'Mum, Dad—this is Jodi Knight. Jodi, my parents.' Griff's introduction was plain and straightforward, understandably giving no qualification of their relationship. She might just be some charity case brought home by the lord of the manor, she thought pettishly, and then was shocked at her own ingratitude. But she still wished he had been less ambiguous, that he had introduced her at the very least as his friend.

'It's very good of you to invite us at such short notice,' she told Mrs Griffiths shyly as she followed her into the house, Griff, his father and Mrs Monkton bringing up the rear with Robin.

'Heavens!' Mrs Griffiths' eyes were still on Tanya's rosy face. 'Goodness doesn't come into it—but pure selfishness. As my son has probably told you, there'll be no children in the house this Christmas—the first I can remember for ages—so these two will be a godsend. Christmas just isn't the same without children.'

Now a maidservant did appear, in order to show Jodi to a guest room. But Mrs Griffiths insisted on taking charge of Tanya and Robin herself. 'Time for afternoon tea, I think, and I can guess just what this young man would like. Join us when you've freshened up, Miss Knight.'

Was that or was it not a hint that Mrs Griffiths had noted her dishevelled state? Jodi wondered as she followed the maid up an impressively broad flight of stairs, overlooked by tall stained-glass windows, through which the wintry afternoon sunshine cast a myriad colours on the fabric and furnishings of the vast entrance hall.

The bedroom, allocated to her alone, would have held a dormitory of girls at Jodi's old boarding-school. And as for the four-poster bed... She was feeling more and more out of her depth, more and more certain that she was not the sort Mr and Mrs Griffiths would want associating with their eldest son.

She unpacked hastily. Her belongings looked lost in the vast wardrobe, but at least the clothes she had brought with her would show she was not normally so unkempt. She showered in an adjoining, surprisingly modern bathroom, then put on a dress which although of a deceptively simple cut had in fact been an expensive buy. 'Quality always shows' had been a maxim learned from her father, one by which she tried to abide when buying stock for the boutique. She had fallen so in love with this particular dress that she had kept it for herself.

As she descended the stairs she was pleasantly conscious of fresh, dainty underwear and the frou-frou of a full petticoat beneath her swirling skirts.

Griff came across the hall to meet her, and the expression in his eyes told her her efforts had not been wasted. He took her elbow in a warm clasp. 'I thought

I'd better wait and show you the way. Visitors often get lost.'

'I'm not surprised,' Jodi said as he ushered her along a maze of interconnecting passageways, some of them on totally different levels, so that one moment they were descending a couple of steps, another mounting a flight of three or four.

'We're having tea in my mother's sitting-room,' Griff explained. 'She thought it would be less formal.'

'Less formal for whom?' Jodi asked suspiciously. Did his mother expect her to reappear still in her jeans?

'For Robin, of course.' He sounded surprised that she needed to ask. 'She wants the children to feel at home.'

Mrs Griffiths' sitting-room might be considered by her family to be less formal, but it was still pretty impressive, Jodi thought. The furnishings, though in keeping with the age and architecture of the house, were by no means old or shabby, and a great deal of thought and money must have gone into their arrangement. The tall windows which extended the full width of one wall commanded a view of a rear garden which must be quite spectacular in summer. Even now, with snow softening its lines, the layout combined elegance with beauty. Heaven only knew how many hours of labour it must take to keep it that way.

'Do you have a garden, Miss Knight?' Mrs Griffiths asked, when Jodi passed a complimentary remark on the outlook.

'No. I live in a flat.'

'So you won't know anything about gardening?'

'No, but I——'

'Do you ride, Miss Knight?' Mr Griffiths asked.

'No, I'm afraid not.' Jodi found herself almost apologising for the fact. She was not accustomed to feeling so inadequate, and once again she was beginning to wish she had resisted Griff's invitation to visit his family home.

'Pity. David could have shown you the rest of the estate on horseback. It's far too extensive to walk, of course, even if ground conditions were suitable.'

For a moment Jodi wondered who on earth 'David' was. Then Griff said, 'We could always take the Range Rover instead. That's if Jodi's interested.'

'I'm sure she wouldn't be,' Mrs Griffiths put in before Jodi could speak. 'Because we love our land so much, it's easy to forget that there's nothing more boring to visitors than their hosts' possessions. It's like other people's holiday photos.'

Jodi, who had been on the point of saying she would be extremely interested in exploring the property, bit her lip. To Mrs Griffiths she was just 'a visitor'. It was quite evident that Mrs Griffiths knew nothing about her son's intentions where she was concerned—and if he hadn't even bothered to mention her to his mother his intentions obviously weren't the kind of which she would approve. In fact, it was quite likely that she had someone else in mind for her eldest son. The daughter, perhaps, of some friend, or another, adjoining landowner.

By the time tea was over, Jodi was beginning to feel decidedly surplus to requirements. It was not that anyone appeared to deliberately exclude her, but Griff and his father were deep in discussion concerning either the running of the store or the maintenance of the estate. Not only was Mrs Griffiths monopolising Tanya, but she and Mrs Monkton had obviously known each other a long time and were busy exchanging gossip, while Robin was engrossed in furthering his acquaintance with a lovable King Charles spaniel.

'Don't bother to change again for dinner, Miss Knight,' Mrs Griffiths said as they disappeared to prepare for the evening. 'What you have on now will do quite nicely. I don't suppose you had much time to prepare for a visit.'

As she took the two children upstairs to get them ready for bed, Jodi found herself seething. Earlier she had looked forward to meeting Griff's parents. She'd been prepared to like them and had hoped the liking would be mutual. Mr Griffiths hadn't said much to her, except for the comment about riding. But everything Mrs Griffiths had said so far seemed to imply, if not exactly disapproval, at least complete lack of any interest in her as a person. Perhaps it hadn't even occurred to her that her son might have anything other than a charitable concern for Jodi.

Tanya and Robin were to sleep in a small room—once a dressing-room—that connected with hers. Both were tired and fell asleep almost immediately, leaving her uncomfortably free to examine her own reactions so far to the Griffiths household.

She found she was dreading going down to dinner. With no children to distract her, Mrs Griffiths was bound to pay more attention to her guests, and, if her husband monopolised Griff once more, Jodi might find herself subjected to closer scrutiny, perhaps even to awkward questions.

If only she could be alone with Griff for a while, feel his arms about her, she might find some reassurance as to his feelings for her. But it didn't look as though the holiday would offer any opportunity of that. And, whatever Griff's intentions, he was not the sort to wear his heart on his sleeve in front of his parents or Mrs Monkton, particularly in view of Jodi's recently expressed uncertainty—an uncertainty which he had misunderstood and she had not been allowed to explain.

If afternoon tea had been an informal meal, dinner was a total contrast. The dining-room was vast, the table capable of holding twenty or more people without any discomfort. Griff and his father were in dinner-jackets, and though Mrs Griffiths and Mrs Monkton were not actually in evening dress as such, Jodi wished she had ignored the former's suggestion that she need not change again.

Never mind, there was always tomorrow in which to demonstrate that she was capable of holding her own in society. But at the thought of another day in this stilted atmosphere, she almost groaned aloud.

Griff was seated between Jodi and his mother, and though he certainly did not ignore Jodi, he was on the receiving end of a barrage of questions from Mrs Griffiths which constantly distracted his attention.

'Are you a churchgoer, Miss Knight?' The question from Mr Griffiths, like that about horse riding, came out of the blue, totally unconnected with any former topic of conversation.

'Er—no, not exactly. I only——'

'My husband wants to know because we always go to the midnight service on Christmas Eve,' his wife put in. 'A family tradition—not one you need observe, of course, if you'd rather have an early night.'

Jodi had been about to say that, while she was not a regular attender at any church, she did observe the major festivals such as Easter and Christmas. But now she did not bother to correct the contrary impression. Perhaps she was being unduly sensitive, but the implication to her ears meant that the Griffiths would prefer the expedition to be a family affair.

'It would probably be just as well if I stay here,' she agreed coolly, 'in case the children wake up and are alarmed at being in unfamiliar surroundings.'

The family left the house at eleven o'clock.

'We have a carol service first,' Griff explained. And then, his eyes intent on her face, 'Sure you don't want to come with me?'

There was nothing she would have enjoyed more than standing side by side with Griff in some beautiful old country church, singing the familiar evocative carols. Jodi loved everything to do with this season of the year. But Mrs Griffiths had stressed 'family' tradition—and she was not family. Nor ever likely to be, she thought unhappily, certain that even if Griff *had* offered marriage, which he hadn't, she had made a bad impression on her host and hostess.

'No, I won't come,' she said quietly.

He was short with her. 'Suit yourself.'

She could have gone to bed once she was alone. Mrs Monkton had already retired. But, 'Molly will serve you a hot drink in the drawing-room before you go up,' Mrs Griffiths had said, and it didn't seem polite to let Molly's efforts be wasted.

As she waited for the maid to appear, the telephone rang. At first Jodi hesitated, thinking that a member of staff would surely answer it. But finally, as it continued to ring, she lifted the receiver.

'Hallo, is Griff there?' a husky female voice enquired. And on being informed that he was not, 'Oh,' with evident disappointment, 'I was told he'd be home for Christmas. Look, Molly, be a love, tell him to ring Victoria, will you?' With that the caller rang off, before Jodi could explain that she was not the Griffithses' maid.

Ten minutes later, as Jodi sipped her drink, the telephone rang again. This time she answered it immediately. Molly, when questioned, had volunteered the information that the rest of the staff were attending the midnight service and that she was off to bed, as she had to be up early to attend the first Mass at a Catholic church some distance away, 'So that I'm back in time to help with lunch.'

The voice was female again and the question was the same. 'Oh, damn! Of course, he'll have been roped in for church, poor darling. I'll ring again first thing tomorrow. Just tell him it was Denise, will you?'

Griff, it appeared, Jodi thought grimly, was very popular with the female sex. *Very* popular, since just as she was on the point of going upstairs herself, yet another caller proved to be female, the name this time being Sonia, the message that she would 'see him tomorrow afternoon'.

No wonder Mrs Griffiths had not seen any particular significance in her arrival, Jodi thought as she added the third message to the jotter pad beside the telephone. Griff seemed to be inundated with women friends.

Both children, when she peeped in at them, were still sleeping soundly. As she hung Robin's Christmas stocking on the foot of his bed, by the light of the low-wattage lamp, left burning in case the children should wake, she studied their peaceful innocent faces. She sighed. She loved these children, but she had always looked upon her feelings as the natural affection of an aunt. Tonight, in her new awareness of herself and her feelings for Griff, she recognised hitherto unsuspected maternal stirrings, found herself trying to imagine how her own children would look—hers and Griff's. But she could not picture them—perhaps because their very existence was an impossibility. She might be willing to forgo marriage if that was the way Griff wanted it, but she was still old-fashioned enough to resolve that she would never bring children into the world outside of marriage.

As she removed her make-up and prepared for bed, Jodi fought a losing battle against depression. For nearly a month now, Griff had been pursuing her relentlessly, but she had taken pains to see that her heart eluded capture. Now, just as she had decided she wanted to be caught, she'd discovered that she was by no means the only one in his life.

Accustomed to sleeping in a single bed, Jodi found the four-poster bed comfortable, but far too large for one person. Again, perhaps that would not have bothered her had it not been for her recent experience of sharing a bed with Griff. But in any event, she could not sleep, her restless brain going over and over the events of the day, unable to prevent herself from speculating about the future. There was not only her ambiguous relationship with Griff, there was also the uncertainty about her business hanging over her. At least when she and Rodney had broken up she had had her work to fall back on.

As she lay there wide-eyed in the dark, she was very much aware of the stirrings of the old building, the way its ancient timbers creaked as, the central heating off for the night, the house cooled. To anyone of a more nervous disposition, knowing they were virtually alone in the house, it could have been a sinister, disturbing noise. Jodi told herself firmly that she was not nervous.

Her bedroom overlooked the front of the house, and she heard the churchgoers returning, their voices, though suitably muted, carrying on the still, frosty air. There came the sounds of people ascending the main staircase. Impossible to do so soundlessly as the treads responded protestingly to pressure. Doors opened and closed. Water gurgled in pipes.

Jodi was just drifting into sleep when something brought her instantly awake, every sense alert. Someone was in her room. Her first reaction was one of amused relief. Of course, it was probably her nephew, disturbed by the night noises of the house.

'Robin?' she said softly. She sat up, fumbling for the bedside light, but with so wide a bed found it out of reach. And then she realised that the weight which had settled itself on the side of her bed was too heavy for any child.

'Jodi?'

'Griff? What on earth——?' At last she found the switch and snapped on the light, blinking in the sudden brightness. Then, her eyes focusing, she discovered him, clad only—so far as she could see—in a brief silky robe.

His eyes, the direction of his gaze, made her realise that sitting up had caused the bedclothes to fall away and that she was revealing far too much creamy flesh to his interested observation. Flushing, she tugged the sheet higher.

'What are you doing here?' she whispered, in a lower key now, very much aware of the children sleeping in the next room, their door left ajar.

'I wanted to be the first to wish you a Merry Christmas, while the day is still young.' But the expression in his eyes told her that he had other things besides the season's greetings on his mind.

'Wh-what time is it?'

'Two o'clock.' Then, huskily, 'To hell with the time. Come here.' For her search for the lamp had taken her to the opposite side of the bed.

A quiver ran through her, a sharp shaft of eroticism, but she shook her head. 'No. You shouldn't be here, Griff.'

'Why, for heaven's sake?' At her refusal to move, he had stood up and walked round the bed, so that only an undignified scramble could remove her from his vicinity.

'Several reasons,' she told him. She wasn't thinking specifically of the telephone messages she had taken earlier, though they lurked below the surface of her refusal. 'The children are only just through there,' she pointed out.

'Is that all?' Griff moved to the communicating door and closed it. 'They won't be disturbed now.' He advanced towards her once more, his expression signalling his intentions all too clearly.

'No, Griff—please. Go away. This isn't right—not under your parents' roof. They think badly enough of me already.'

This halted him. 'What on earth are you talking about?' he demanded.

'It was quite obvious to me,' she told him, 'so I'm surprised it wasn't obvious to you— I'm like a fish out of water here. I just don't fit in.'

'Rubbish!' He approached the bed once more and sat down again, taking both her hands in his. He raised her hands to his lips and began a gentle nuzzling of each finger. 'It's wonderful having you here,' he murmured.

'It isn't rubbish,' she insisted. 'Oh, they were perfectly polite to me, but they couldn't have made it clearer if they'd spelt it out. I made a bad impression from the moment I walked in, looking like a scarecrow. Stop it, Griff!' For he had turned her hands over now and was pressing little kisses into her palm, against her wrists, and the caress was having a devastating effect on her senses.

He foiled her attempts to snatch her hands away. 'Jodi, will you stop talking nonsense and concentrate on more important things?' His grasp tightened and he tried to pull her towards him, but she resisted fiercely.

'I wasn't dressed right, I know nothing about gardening. I can't ride—and clearly I wasn't wanted at your family church parade tonight. And don't try to laugh it off.' For Griff was shaking his head, a distinct curve to his lips.

'At least all this angst shows that you care—that you'd like to belong. But, Jodi, you're reading far too much into casual conversation. It wasn't some kind of inquisition or a test of your suitability.'

'I don't believe you. Why,' she added indignantly, 'your parents didn't even use my first name. It was ''Miss Knight'' all the time.'

Griff sighed with exasperation as once again his attempts to bring her closer were prevented.

'So my parents come of a generation that finds informality difficult. Give them a chance—another day and they'll be using your name without any self-consciousness.'

'I'm not sure I want to stay another day,' she muttered.

The affectionate impatience vanished and his brow creased into a frown. 'You'd seriously consider depriving the children of their Christmas pleasure? Just because you seem to have some kind of inferiority complex—quite unjustifiably so—where my parents are concerned?'

'Griff,' she pleaded, 'I don't think it is unjustifiable. Women have a kind of sixth sense about these things that men don't seem to share—an intuition. I just know your parents don't——'

'I still think you're totally wrong. But forget my parents for the moment. You're here because *I* want you here—and you're wasting time with all this discussion—time,' huskily, 'that we could spend far more enjoyably.'

His hands were on either side of her face now and his lips came down on hers, stifling her protests. But even so she fought him, pummelling his shoulders, pushing at them, refusing to return his kiss until at last he drew away.

'For God's sake, what's the matter with you, Jodi?' he demanded.

'I know what you're trying to do, and I won't sleep with you under your parents' roof without their knowledge.'

'Would you like me to go and tell them—and ask their permission?' he snapped sarcastically.

'Don't be ridiculous. You know what I mean.'

'You're the one who's being ridiculous. Letting an imagined slight—and it *is* all in your imagination— come between us.'

'It's not just that. It would be an abuse of their hospitality. I have certain standards. But perhaps you don't,' said Jodi. 'How many other women have you made love to in this bed? Have *they* all slept here?'

'Who?' Griff's tone was grim. 'Have who slept here?'

'Your three other girlfriends.'

He leaned forward and put a hand on her forehead. 'You're not feverish,' he muttered.

'No, I'm not, and I'm not naïve either. When three different women phone here, one after another, all very anxious to speak to you—devastated because you're not here, I can draw my own conclusions.'

'Can you?' He was sarcastic again. 'Perhaps you think you can. But I——'

'Auntie Jodi?'

In the heat of the argument they had forgotten to keep their voices low, and now the adjoining door opened to reveal a small tousle-headed Robin, rubbing sleep from his eyes.

'It's all right, darling,' Jodi reassured him, 'I'm here. Did we wake you? I'm sorry.'

As the small boy stumbled across the room and clambered on to the bed, Griff turned on his heel.

'For your information, I wasn't intending to climb into your bed. Oh, I admit I came here hoping for a little show of affection, but that was all. I too have "standards", as you put it. We'll finish this discussion some other time,' he threw at her over his shoulder, 'when you're in a more rational frame of mind.'

CHAPTER SIX

JODI hadn't the heart to take the small boy back to his own bed, and after a few sleepy questions about 'Where's Mummy?' and 'Has Father Christmas been yet?', Robin fell asleep beside her.

But Jodi lay awake for a long time after he slept. Griff's visit to her room, his words, his kisses, had left her far more agitated than she had let him see. She ached to be held in his arms, to feel his strong body pressed to hers, to know again the heady intimacy of his lovemaking.

If only she did not have these doubts about his parents' reception of her, if only there had not been those three revealing telephone calls, she would not have been so coldly dismissive of him.

Yet despite all this her body had reacted in what had become a familiar excitement to his touch. Those fleeting but erotic kisses on her hands and wrists had brought life to senses which now refused to subside.

Allowing him to make love to her that one time had been sheer foolishness on her part, a strong physical attraction overcoming good sense, and now she must pay the penalty for that foolishness—for she realised now that intimacy, once experienced, left an intolerable void which could only be filled by constant repetition of what it craved.

But her situation here was impossible. Inviting someone into your family home could be very testing to a relationship. Despite his denials, pretty soon it would become as obvious to Griff as it was to her that she did not fit in here. And then he would return his attentions to one of the three other contenders.

It was dawn before Jodi's eyes finally closed, and only two hours later when an excited Robin roused her from a heavy, unrefreshing slumber.

'Happy Christmas, darling,' she said when she had cleared her sleep-blurred mind and directed him towards his stocking, bulging with small treasures. All personal tensions and unhappiness must be put aside at least for today, for Robin's sake, and she only hoped that, for the sake of harmony, Griff would not try to take up their discussion where it had left off earlier this morning.

Getting herself and the children washed and dressed, while answering Robin's never-ending questions, necessitated closing her mind against all other considerations, but a sinking feeling in her stomach was all too clear an indication that her subconscious was still aware of unresolved problems.

Initially, she thought that she and the children were first down to breakfast, but 'No,' Molly told her, 'the master and Mr David had their breakfast an hour ago and now they've gone riding. They always do that when Mr David's at home.'

Another 'family' tradition, Jodi thought. 'And Mrs Griffiths?' she asked.

'She's having her breakfast in bed. She doesn't come down much before eleven most mornings.'

Not even when she had guests, apparently—or perhaps she didn't feel her current guests were important enough to warrant a change in her habits. This disquieting train of thought was interrupted by the arrival of Mrs Monkton, who greeted Jodi cheerfully, wishing her a Merry Christmas.

'Have you opened all your parcels yet?' the older woman asked Robin.

'I think Father Christmas has hidden a few more away to be opened later with everyone else,' Jodi smiled.

But her smile faded as Mrs Monkton said, 'Oh, but the Griffiths will have opened theirs last night when they got back from church.'

'A family tradition?' Jodi asked coolly enough. Inwardly, though, she was annoyed. They might have waited, for the children's sake. Tanya was too young to bother, but Robin had been brought up to enjoy watching other people open their parcels as well as opening his own.

'Only of recent years,' Mrs Monkton explained. 'Apparently when the children were little they all gathered round the tree after breakfast. But these last few years, since Mrs Griffiths hasn't been too well, she tends to rise late.'

'She isn't well?' Guilt stabbed Jodi. Her thoughts about Griff's mother to date had been decidedly unflattering.

'Didn't you know? She had a stroke three years ago. She made a marvellous recovery. But she has to be careful.'

Griff and his father returned just as they were finishing breakfast. Both were glowing with the fresh air and exercise and obviously in high good humour with each other.

Jodi had been dreading the first encounter of the day, but from Griff's manner towards her no one

would have suspected that only hours ago they had
been in the throes of a violent disagreement. He
wished her, Mrs Monkton and Robin a Happy
Christmas, and allowed Robin to itemise for him the
fascinating contents of his stocking.

'Why don't we all go into the drawing-room now
and have a look under the tree?' Griff suggested.

'I thought you'd all opened your presents last
night,' Jodi couldn't help remarking.

'Family presents, yes. But there are parcels for the
children, for Mrs M and for you.'

When Jodi had packed hastily yesterday for the visit
to Kent, she had remembered to slip his parcel into
her luggage. It had been bought as a precaution
against embarrassment—in case he gave her one. Now
she made an excuse to go upstairs and get it. She
wasn't really in the mood for exchanging gifts, but
the traditions of the day must be observed.

By the time she returned, Robin was happily divesting various parcels of their wrappings and Mrs
Monkton was 'helping' Tanya with hers. Griff had
been incredibly generous.

Jodi handed him his package, and received one in
return. It was a very small, square box, and she regarded it doubtfully. It looked very much like the
boxes in which jewellers put rings. But it couldn't be
that.

'It's not booby-trapped,' Griff observed. He had
unwrapped and shaken out her impersonally safe
gift—a silk tie.

Her fingers trembled as she removed the paper and
revealed—as she had suspected—a jeweller's box.
Taking a deep steadying breath, she flipped open the

lid, and a small breath of relief escaped her as she saw the earrings.

'Thank you,' she said, and unwisely met his eyes, saw in them an ironic understanding. He knew what she had expected to see, and his expression was telling her those expectations had been groundless.

'How about a stroll in the garden before lunch?' he asked when the presents had all been opened and the wrappings cleared away. 'It's a glorious morning, not too cold, and the gardener has cleared the paths.'

Jodi looked at him incredulously, 'You expect your gardener to work on Christmas Day?'

He raised his eyebrows. 'We have more than one gardener. Any member of staff who has to work Christmas Day is handsomely paid and has Boxing Day off instead.'

'How generous!' she muttered sarcastically. She was feeling decidedly out of charity with the Griffiths family and all their wealth this morning. She felt aggrieved with Griff in particular, otherwise she might have been prepared to acknowledge that there were many occupations which necessitated working at holiday times and that probably the Griffithses' gardener was willing to accept his terms of employment.

'So—are you coming?' Griff sounded impatient. 'We haven't long, and I want to talk to you.'

Their unfinished business from last night, no doubt. This thought had her cravenly seeking an excuse. 'I promised to play Ludo with Robin.'

'I'll play with Robin,' Mrs Monkton said at once. 'I'd love to—I haven't played Ludo for years. You go off and get some fresh air, my dear.'

Jodi could hardly make an issue of refusing, though to be alone with Griff was the last thing she wanted right now. 'I'll go and get my coat,' she said, but she took as long as she dared over this errand. She wouldn't put it past Griff to come in search of her if she delayed too long.

As she descended the stairs he was waiting for her in the hall. She felt extremely self-conscious under his appraising stare.

'You were wearing that coat the very first time I saw you,' he said. 'As I once told you—from that moment——'

'David darling!' He was interrupted by his mother's voice calling him from the landing above.

Looking back up the staircase, Jodi saw Mrs Griffiths leaning over the ornately carved banister. The older woman still wore her housecoat, but hair and make-up were impeccable.

'Morning, Mother.' His attention diverted, he took the stairs two at a time in order to plant a kiss on her cheek. 'Everything OK?' This with an anxious glance.

'Splendid, darling. You all worry too much about me. It's just that Hilary telephoned while you were out. I promised to make sure you called back straight away. But I didn't hear you come in. Molly says you've been in over an hour—and I did promise——'

'No problem,' he assured her. 'I'll call right away.' And to Jodi, 'You won't mind waiting a few moments?'

'Oh, no, not at all,' she said with icy sweetness. 'Why not call the other three while you're at it?'

A darkling look promised retribution later for that crack, and as Griff disappeared into the library to use the extension there Jodi decided on a swift retreat. And since she was already dressed for outdoors...

She slipped out of a side-door and found herself in the vast formal garden which, she discovered, extended around the house. As Griff had promised, the paths that made an intricate geometric pattern had been cleared of snow. But this was too tame an amble for Jodi in her present frame of mind. She had also donned a serviceable pair of boots, and now she strode out determinedly, making for a wooded area which formed the boundary between the garden and the rest of the estate.

Overnight, frost had crisped the surface of the snow and a pleasant crunchy noise accompanied each step. There was a little warmth in the pale sunlight. In fact, it was an altogether pleasant and invigorating walk, and in any other circumstances Jodi would have been thoroughly enjoying herself.

'So it's Hilary this time, is it?' she muttered aloud. 'Victoria, Denise, Sonia and now Hilary. I wonder just how many more there are? And Sonia will even be turning up this afternoon. That should be interesting.'

Her pace brought her swiftly to the wooded area that was her goal, and she plunged in among the trees. The density of the evergreens meant that very little snow had penetrated the overhead canopy and the going became easier. Perhaps if she walked fast enough and far enough, Griff would not bother to come after her. If she could avoid him until lunchtime...

She must have been walking through the woods for nearly an hour when she realised that she was lost. She had not expected the woodland to be so extensive, and with no snow underfoot she could not retrace the way by following her own tracks.

A glance at her watch told her it was now past the hour appointed for lunch. Damn. Her tardiness was hardly likely to endear her to her host and hostess.

Then another devastating thought occurred to her. Griff had promised to drive her into London later this afternoon, for visiting time at the hospital. If she couldn't find her way back to the house in time... Sally would think her sister so engrossed in her own pursuits that she had forgotten all about her.

Desperately she ploughed on, the boots which she rarely wore chafing her feet now, her legs aching with their extra weight. Once or twice she stumbled, tripping over tree roots, and then finally she fell heavily, feeling her knee twist painfully as she did so.

Winded, she lay for a moment getting her breath back and waiting for the agonising pain in her knee to subside. It did not do so. And when, after a few more moments, she attempted to rise she found it impossible. At the same moment that she realised she was totally incapable of standing up, a fresh stab of pain made everything go black and she passed out.

'Jodi! Jodi?'

She regained consciousness hazily, painfully, to see Griff on his knees beside her, his face anxious. His hands, she discovered, were chafing hers, which she realised were as cold as ice. How long had she been here?

'What in God's name were you playing at?' he demanded, anger showing through now as he realised she was not after all deeply unconscious.

'I tripped,' she said, biting her lip as an unwary movement set her leg throbbing again. 'I seem to have wrenched my knee. I can't stand.'

He sighed exasperatedly. 'If you hadn't gone tearing off at half-cock on your own, this would never have happened. Now I suppose I'll have to carry you.'

Well, he needn't sound as if he found the chore so distasteful.

'Don't bother,' she snapped, pain and irritation making her peevish, 'just send one of your menials to fetch me. No doubt you'll pay them handsomely for it!'

'I'm in no mood right now for sparring with you.' Grim-faced, he took hold of her, rising to his feet all in the same movement, and Jodi found herself encased by steely arms against a hard chest. The sudden closeness made her heart flutter erratically in her chest, but his breathing seemed hardly disturbed by his exertions as he strode homeward, finding his way with unerring accuracy along tracks that looked identical to her.

'What on earth got into you?' he demanded. 'Why didn't you wait for me? You knew I wanted to talk to you.'

'I'm not in the habit of standing round waiting for men while they phone a string of other girlfriends.'

She was not looking at him as she spoke or she might have seen a glimmer of humour in his face as he said, 'Actually, I only called Hilary. I rang the others earlier this morning, before I went out.'

'You must have had a lot to say to Hilary,' she retorted acidly, 'it took you long enough.'

'We did have a lot to talk about,' he agreed.

His quiet complacency infuriated her still further. 'I think it would be best if the children and I went back to London this afternoon,' she told him. 'It was a mistake to bring us here.'

'Nonsense!' His grip tightened. 'You haven't given things a chance yet. Besides, the children are enjoying themselves.'

'Well, I'm not.'

'That's entirely your own fault.' And before she could frame an indignant reply, 'Due chiefly to your suspicious nature and over-developed imagination.'

'Imagination! Huh! I suppose I imagined all those phone calls?'

'Not at all.' Griff grinned suddenly. 'And I must say I find all this jealousy very promising.'

'Jealousy? What on earth makes you think I'm jealous? I couldn't care less,' she lied, 'how many female friends you have, or how many of them come to see you while I'm here. Let them all come, for all I care!'

'Oh, Jodi!' His face, his disbelieving smile was very close, his eyes on her pursed lips. 'If only it weren't getting so late——'

'Oh, yes, about that—I'm sorry if I've kept you from your Christmas dinner,' she said, hastily averting her head. Something had put it into her mind that he was about to kiss her.

'No problem! We don't eat our main meal until evening, and lunch has been put back. One of the advantages,' he added with deliberate irony, 'of having a good—and well paid—household staff.'

'Put back? Because of me? Oh, heavens!' Jodi exclaimed.

They had almost reached the house now, and uncomfortable as she was in such close proximity to Griff, she was dreading even more the coming encounter with Mr and Mrs Griffiths. Despite Griff's disclaimer, they were bound to be put out at the inconvenience she had caused them.

'My parents were extremely anxious for your safety—and besides, they didn't want you to miss your meal,' Griff told her.

Jodi was silent. But she couldn't believe the Griffithses could care two hoots. It was probably just their innate sense of courtesy—a quality they would be bound to think she lacked.

'So,' he went on cheerfully, 'since you've met with an accident, as we feared—though luckily not too serious—after lunch, I'll take you in to see your sister, and at the same time we'll visit Casualty and get that knee looked at.'

And after that...? 'Look, Griff, I meant what I said,' she told him. 'Let's take the children with us and you can drop us back in Hampstead afterwards. This has all been a terrible mistake—as much on my part as yours. I should never have agreed——'

'And how do you think you'd go on, looking after two small children, when you've damaged your knee and might very well have to rest it? No, Jodi, whether you like it or not, you're coming back here—for as long as it's necessary.'

'Necessary for what? My leg will probably be perfectly all right by tomorrow.'

'I'm not just referring to your leg,' he said darkly.

But by this time they were in the vast hall and she was being exclaimed over by the Griffithses and Mrs Monkton. And she was still apologising for all the inconvenience she had caused when Griff carried her out to the car for the journey to London.

'Now will you believe that my parents aren't entirely indifferent to you?' he said as they drove away.

Their manner certainly had seemed warmer, their concern unaffected. Her apologies had been received gracefully and disclaimed as being totally unnecessary.

'I enjoyed my food all the better for eating later,' Mrs Griffiths had declared. 'I'm afraid I breakfast rather late these days.'

'I don't see why they should care particularly about me,' Jodi said. 'I've intruded on a family holiday. As a guest I've proved to be a damned nuisance, and besides, I'm only one of a string of——'

'They care because I've told them how much you mean to me,' Griff said, taking her breath away momentarily.

'But we're not...I mean...I said...'

'Oh, I know what you said. But I'm not accepting that as final.'

Jodi was silent. Wasn't this what she had hoped for—that he would show his usual persistence? But that was before she had seen his lifestyle, discovered just how many women were vying for his attention. Wealthy men invariably had a playboy image, and she hadn't known Griff very long. Would she feel able to trust him? She didn't want a repetition of her experience with Rodney.

'What?' Griff exclaimed. 'Lost your tongue? No more arguments? Or does silence imply consent?'

'Griff, I——'

'No, don't say anything now. I can tell from your expression, your tone of voice, that I shan't like what you're going to say. We'll discuss this when you're in a more amenable frame of mind. Perhaps a little Christmas spirit will mellow you.'

*   *   *

Griff carried her into the hospital. But, once her knee had been X-rayed and strapped up, he used a hospital wheelchair to take her to the maternity ward.

'Sally! Oh, Sally, how are you?' It was such a relief to see her sister sitting up in bed and looking her usual cheerful self.

'What have you been doing to yourself?' Sally wanted to know.

'Oh, just a stupid accident—twisted my knee. Never mind about me. You had me frightened out of my wits,' Jodi went on as she handed over the flowers she had purchased in the hospital's florist shop and hugged her sister, but carefully, having regard for her delicate state.

'Me too,' Sally admitted. 'But I'm fine now, honestly. In fact, with all the painkillers I feel quite euphoric. But I feel so guilty about leaving you in the lurch, and at Christmas too. How on earth are you coping—especially now you've hurt your knee? It won't be much of a Christmas for you.'

'On the contrary,' Griff said, 'I hope this is going to be the most memorable Christmas in Jodi's life.'

'Oh?' Sally looked from one to the other with palpable curiosity. 'Does that mean——?'

'What Griff means,' Jodi said hastily, 'is that he's kindly invited me and the children to stay with his family over the holiday. So you don't need to worry about us. Just concentrate on getting your strength back. Can I have a peep at my new nephew?' she asked, hoping to steer the conversation firmly away from herself and Griff.

She bent over the cot. 'Isn't he just perfect?' she enthused. 'He looks just like Robin did at this age.'

'I haven't had much chance to study him,' Sally admitted. 'I've been doped to the eyeballs most of the time. They just brought him in ready for visiting.' And, excitedly, 'Oh, Jodi, Barry called the hospital. He's on his way, and in view of the circumstances they're letting him stay in England for a whole fortnight. Isn't it fabulous? I can't wait to see him.'

'I'm so glad for you,' Jodi said sincerely, but she couldn't repress a stab of envy at the evidence of so much domestic bliss. How ironic that was. Only a couple of weeks ago she had been vaunting her preference for personal freedom.

'Now that I've said hello and congratulations,' Griff told Sally, 'I'll leave you two alone for a while. I'm sure you've got some girl talk to indulge in.'

Jodi didn't know which was worse, having Griff there with Sally's speculative eye upon them, with the risk that she might come out with some embarrassing remark about their relationship, or being left alone with Sally, which gave her sister a chance to exercise her curiosity.

'So you've been introduced to the family,' Sally said as soon as the swing door had closed behind Griff. 'Sounds a promising development. Wedding bells next?'

Jodi shook her head. 'Don't read too much into it, Sal. I'm not. They're a very religious family. They probably see it as their Christian duty to rescue three waifs and strays at Christmas.'

Sally looked at her quizzically. 'Do I detect an embittered note? Don't you like them? And do you mean to tell me Griff isn't making the most of his opportunities, having you under his roof? If so, he's not half the man I took him for.'

'Oh, Sal, if only it were that simple. But there are too many problems. If only you knew.'

'Why not tell me about it?' her sister suggested. 'The problems might be only in your mind. You always were a one for making mountains out of molehills.'

Jodi gave her a brief résumé of events.

'And Griff says it's all your imagination?' Sally mused. 'I'm inclined to believe him, you know. You have been hyper-sensitive since the Rodney affair. As to all these women who keep phoning him—Griff may just be one of these men who are capable of remaining on friendly terms with their exes. Why on earth don't you just ask him?'

'Because I won't give him the satisfaction of thinking I'm jealous. And perhaps I'm afraid of the answers.'

'You don't seriously believe that Griff is juggling a positive harem of women? That he wants to add you to it? That he's a bed-hopper?'

'No...yes...oh, I don't know what to think,' sighed Jodi. 'I've never been so confused in my life.'

Sally grinned. 'Love gets you that way. If you want my advice, just hang on in there over the holiday, keep your eyes and ears open and your mouth shut. You may find out a lot that way, and also save yourself from saying something you'll regret later.'

'I just hope,' Jodi said soberly, 'that I'm not going to have cause to regret the whole thing.'

Sally looked at her keenly. 'You don't mean...? You can tell me to mind my own business if you like, but you are my little sister...and you did spend a whole night with him. I take it you did...?' She paused delicately, and as Jodi reluctantly nodded, 'You don't by any chance mean you might be pregnant?'

'I don't know—yet,' Jodi admitted. 'There hasn't been time to——'

'So neither of you took precautions?'

Jodi shook her head. 'It all happened in the heat of the moment.'

'Oh, my God!' Sally regarded her exasperatedly. 'If anyone had asked me I'd have said at least that you were street-wise. If you are, will you tell him?'

'I don't know,' Jodi said miserably. 'But probably not. It would seem like blackmailing him into some kind of commitment.'

'Well, let's not cross that bridge until we have to. You might have been lucky this time. Just don't let him get you into bed again until things are resolved between you.'

Griff came in again briefly at the end of visiting time to say goodbye to Sally, and to wheel Jodi out, promising to bring her again next day. 'And perhaps you'd like Robin to come too?' he suggested. 'Or won't you be feeling up to a lively small boy?'

'Oh, I'd love him to come, if it's not too much trouble. I miss them both dreadfully.' Sally was suddenly tearful, and Jodi was feeling so low-spirited that her own eyes pricked in sympathy.

'Of course we'll bring him,' she said. 'We'll bring both of them. And Barry might be here by then,' she added encouragingly.

Griff seemed very quiet and thoughtful on the journey back into Kent, and Jodi was only too thankful to be silent. She had feared another confrontation once they were alone again, but perhaps Griff had decided she was still not in the right frame of mind. And when they reached his parents' home it was time to go upstairs, put the children to bed and prepare herself for the evening's festivities.

And this evening, Jodi decided grimly, she would give them the works. Hanging in the wardrobe was the evening dress she had packed for the holiday, and though she was not given to narcissism she knew she looked good in it. Simply, almost severely cut in black with shoestring shoulder-straps and plunging necklines front and back, it set off her creamy skin and silvery fairness, emphasising her wand-like slenderness, cupping breasts surprisingly full for her slight figure.

With her smooth skin she needed very little make-up, just a touch of lipstick and eyeshadow to enhance large grey eyes. She wore no adornment other than her usual wristwatch and a long pair of silver earrings.

Griff had promised to come up and fetch her down, but her knee felt much easier and she was determined not to give him the opportunity to hold her so closely. It did nothing for her defences. Cautiously, she essayed the stairs.

The family were to gather in the drawing-room for pre-dinner drinks, and, despite the awareness of looking her best, Jodi paused on the threshold to take a steadying breath before entering.

Griff and his parents were chatting over their drinks, and it was Mrs Monkton who noticed her first, interrupting their conversation in mid-flow.

'My dear, how very lovely you look.'

This had the effect of drawing all eyes upon her, and as one Griff and his father moved towards her, echoing the compliment.

But it was Griff who took her arm. 'I told you I'd carry you downstairs,' he said as he steered her towards the blazing log fire and the drinks tray set out on a low table before it.

'I'm perfectly able to manage,' she told him. 'There's——'

'I was just about to say, David, when Jodi came in,' Mrs Griffiths went on as if there had been no interruption, 'that Sonia was very disappointed to miss you this afternoon. She seems very anxious to see you as soon as possible and was very mysterious about it.'

Griff smiled. 'That's Sonia all over.' He turned to Jodi. 'What will you have to drink?' And he reeled off a long list of suggestions.

Jodi muttered something, hardly noticing what it was she drank. So Sonia had not been put off by Griff's absence with another woman—if she even knew he was with another woman. Perhaps Mrs Griffiths was as adept at juggling her son's girlfriends as he was.

Dinner was a very intimate meal, with just the five of them assembled round a small table set up purposely for the occasion.

'I couldn't bear the thought of the larger table with all those empty spaces this year,' Mrs Griffiths explained. 'I know the children have to visit their other grandparents occasionally, but I do wish they hadn't all chosen to do it at the same time.'

'Never mind, Mum,' Griff said bracingly. 'You see them all nearly every other weekend of the year.'

'Yes, but,' stubbornly, 'Christmas is different.'

'I'm afraid this isn't very exciting for you young people,' Mr Griffiths said after dinner when they had repaired to yet another room, the television-room in this case. 'I daresay your mother and I and Mrs Monkton will be content to view all evening, but you two mustn't feel bound to sit it out.'

'Thanks, Dad,' Griff said. 'I must admit I'm not over-enamoured of television—too many repeats. This might be a good opportunity to show Jodi the rest of the house.' And to Jodi, 'It has a very interesting history and some unusual nooks and crannies, including a priest's hole. Would you be interested?'

Jodi was just about to say she would be quite happy to watch television—not because she was addicted to viewing either but because the alternative meant being alone with Griff—and she knew her weaknesses where he was concerned. But she was not allowed to demur.

'Of course she'll enjoy that better,' Mr Griffiths said. 'Off you go now.'

'I . . . I ought to look in on the children,' Jodi said as they left the room, hoping to delay the moment when they would be entirely alone.

'No need. Molly's checking on them from time to time. She's quite reliable. Relax, Jodi, enjoy the break. Now, where shall we start?' But it was a purely rhetorical question, because Griff went on, 'You've seen most of this wing and there's nothing of particular interest in the east wing—that's mostly storage and servants' quarters. So, the west wing it is.' He took her hand and led her through a door she had not noticed before, and then, before she could protest, swept her into his arms to carry her up a second, less imposing flight of stairs.

Held in his arms, his breath lightly fanning her cheek, the scent of him—composed of male warmth and his tangy aftershave—coming to her nostrils, Jodi felt the old familiar desire stir within her. Oh, if only this were their home and Griff was carrying her upstairs to their bedroom.

'Are you cold?' Griff must have felt her sensuous shiver. 'This old house can be a bit draughty at times.'

'N-no, I'm fine.'

His quizzical look told her that having eliminated the most obvious cause of that shudder, he now knew as well as she did what had caused it, and his arms tightened.

'Don't try to deny what you are, Jodi. The Sleeping Beauty has finally woken up, and she won't be put back to sleep again.'

Jodi swallowed, the nerves in the pit of her stomach clenching tightly against the sensations sweeping through her.

'Strictly speaking, the west wing is my territory when I'm home, but it also gets used when the house is full to bursting,' Griff told her as they reached the first floor. 'It's fully self-contained—all the rooms are furnished.' So saying, he threw open a heavy, panelled door and carried her into a drawing-room, smaller and of cosier proportions than that in the main house.

To her surprise a log fire burned strongly in the grate, and set out on a low table was a tray holding a coffee pot, a plate of mince pies and a decanter and two glasses.

Jodi looked at him questioningly and he smiled wryly, 'Yes, this *was* all planned in advance. And I've given orders that we're not to be disturbed.'

'You were taking things a bit for granted,' she said indignantly, pride necessitating the protest. 'I could have refused. I could have stayed with your parents.'

'Oh,' he said huskily, 'I would have found some way to change your mind. I've been wanting to be alone with you ever since we got here.' He moved towards the old-fashioned but comfortable-looking settee pulled up before the fire—far too comfortable-looking and with room only for two—and those two in close proximity.

'I . . . I'd rather not sit so near to the fire,' Jodi said hastily, looking around her for an alternative seat, but the matching armchairs were already occupied by two extremely large cats.

'I'll pull the settee back a bit.' Griff set her down, then suited his actions to the words. 'Sit down, Jodi.' It was a command rather than an invitation.

'I hope you haven't brought me up here just to continue this afternoon's argument,' she said—then blushed furiously, in case that sounded as though she was quite willing to partake in some other activity.

He seemed to find the words and the blush amusing. 'Coffee? Or a drink?' he asked, his hands hovering over the tray.

'Coffee,' she said shortly. She could have done with something stronger to steady her nerves, but she needed to keep her wits about her. From this moment on she would be fighting not just Griff but her own growing, painful need for him.

'Pity,' his smile was one of pure wickedness, 'I was hoping to imbue you with a little Christmas spirit.'

'I know what you were hoping. But I'm not that naïve, Griff.' She cast around desperately for a change of subject. 'Anyway, I thought we were supposed to be looking at the rest of the house.'

'Plenty of time for that,' significantly, 'afterwards.' He handed her the coffee, but did not bother pouring one for himself. Instead he sat back, the movement bringing his shoulders and thighs into far too close a proximity to hers. She could feel his warmth, penetrating the thin material of her dress and against her bare arm. It took a heroic effort to restrain the sensuous shudder that ran through her.

'Afterwards?' she echoed suspiciously.

He turned to look at her, his eyes gravely intent. 'Oh, come on, Jodi.' His finger traced the curve of her cheek, moved on to outline her mouth—an innocent gesture yet subtly imbued with deeper meaning so that her breasts rose and fell on a quick little breath. 'You know we can't go on like this,' he murmured throatily, 'me trying to make love to you, you sniping at me from behind that iron curtain of yours.' He leaned towards her and slid an arm about her shoulders, trying to draw her closer, but she resisted.

'Griff, I...I told you, I don't want to discuss our...our relationship now—here. Since...since we came here I'm discovering new things about you. I need time to think—on my own ground.'

'We've met on your territory many times,' he pointed out. 'Now it's my turn. Surely, just because I'm in my parents' home, I haven't suddenly turned into an unfamiliar monster? I'm still the same man who made love to you...who wants very much to make love to you again. Jodi!' His hands cupped her face and he murmured her name coaxingly.

Despite herself her insides turned over and her hand began to shake, rattling her cup in its saucer. With a little murmur Griff took her untouched coffee from her and set it down.

The next moment she was in his arms, and this time he was not taking no for an answer, and struggle as she might there was no escaping him. But even as she struggled she knew it was only a token protest. Whatever her mind might be screaming about folly, her body was in charge now and—like Griff—would brook no denial of its needs.

Even so, 'Griff, no, you're hurting me,' she protested faintly against his lips.

His clasp did not relax one iota. 'I've tried being patient with you,' he told her, 'and gentle. There's a time for patience and gentleness and there's a time for stronger measures. I've decided that time has come.'

'Griff! N——' Her words were cut off by his mouth as ruthlessly it covered hers, demanding, forcing a response from her.

And she was not long in giving him that response. He knew only too well his devastating effect on her, damn him. His mouth on hers, his long hard body pressed against her, those seeking, coaxing hands were more than human flesh and blood could withstand. And these last few weeks had proved to her that she *was* only human.

The intimate throbbing of her own body, her spinning senses, told the tale of her total vulnerability to him. From that first stiff token resistance she went limp in his arms, but only for a moment. For then her own restless desires made her body as urgent as his, pressing against him, moving agitatedly with her need. Her arms wound about his neck, she returned his kisses, her parted lips welcoming his tongue's invasion as eagerly as her body urged a deeper, more intimate invasion.

And then somehow they were no longer on the settee but were sliding, still entwined, on to the deep pile of the hearthrug, the fire warm upon them, but no warmer than their striving bodies as they clung and touched.

Jodi was dimly aware of the narrow straps sliding from her shoulders, the silky dress offering no resistance as Griff peeled it from her quivering body.

The firelight played and danced its flickering shadows on their naked flesh as they lay closely enmeshed.

'God, but you're beautiful!' Griff paused long enough between kisses to sweep his burning gaze over her, from head to foot.

Somewhere deep in her subconscious a little voice was telling her that this was madness, that she should put a stop to this right now. But the little voice was drowned in the waves of desire sweeping through her, and she gave herself up gladly to his possession, her urgency matching his. Again and again they made love, with seemingly inexhaustible appetites, falling asleep finally in each other's arms, the fire burning lower and lower until only the last red glow remained.

CHAPTER SEVEN

'WHAT on earth was that?'

It was the sound of an indignant yowl that woke Jodi from her deep exhausted slumber. She shivered. The rug Griff had pulled over them just before they slept had slipped away from her so that he appeared to be monopolising it. The lights still burned, but the fire had long since gone out and the room struck a chill to her naked flesh. But not as cold as the icy chill she felt as she remembered what had happened last night.

Once more the crazy pull of sexual attraction had overcome common sense, and she had succumbed mindlessly to its lure. She had asked none of the questions she had been determined to put to Griff, about the other women in his life. She had also intended to make it quite clear to him that while she might be prepared to go along with the modern trend for permanent relationships outside marriage—if that was what he wanted—she was not interested in a transitory affair.

She sat up, and a glance at her wristwatch told her it was after three in the morning. She looked around the room, seeking the source of the noise that had disturbed her. Then she saw that one of the cats had decided it was time for his night-time perambulations and was scratching vigorously at the carpet by the closed door.

Cautiously, so as not to disturb Griff, she stood up, gathering her clothes as she did so. Pausing only to pull on her brief panties and slide the silky dress back over her head, she opened the door for the cat and slipped through it herself, praying that in this rabbit warren of a house she would be able to find her way back to her own room.

'Not so fast!' A hand snaked around her waist.

'Oh!' Startled, Jodi spun round, trying to shake off the encircling grasp. Griff must have the reactions of the predatory feline whose escape she had just assisted, for she had not heard him move across the thickly carpeted floor. And somehow in those few seconds he had also found time to pull on his trousers. Now he stood right behind her, tall and darkly disturbing. Her tongue cleaved to the roof of her mouth and it was an effort to speak. 'I . . . I thought you were still asleep.'

'Obviously,' he said grimly. His grasp shifted to her arm and tightened until she felt he might crush her bones as he pulled her back into the room and closed the door. 'Just what did you think you were up to?'

'I was going to my own room.'

'Why?' he demanded peremptorily.

Why had she suddenly decided she must escape? She wasn't really sure herself. Unless it was the craven impulse to avoid the inevitable confrontation—because she had to tell him—ask him . . .

'I don't have to give you a reason,' she said sharply. 'Or ask your permission.'

'OK, but why wander round the house in the dead of night when there's a perfectly good bed through there?' He pointed to an adjoining door.

Jodi was having trouble breathing and her heart was thudding painfully, but she must stand firm. 'Because I'm not going to share your bed. I——'

'I suppose,' silkily, 'next you'll be telling me—yet again—that last night should never have happened.'

Her lips were dry and she wetted them nervously with her tongue. 'It . . . it shouldn't. I didn't mean it to. I never intended to become one of your . . . your harem.'

'My what?' he rapped out, his eyes dangerously narrowed.

'You know damned well what I mean.' The names seemed to swell in her throat, suffocating her. 'Victoria, Denise, Sonia, Hilary . . . What the hell are you laughing at?' For he had attempted to speak and then choked on his words.

'So you're still on about that! I thought by now you'd have found out . . .'

'Found out what? What else is there to find out, for heaven's sake? A few more names? Have I missed some out?'

'Well, let me see,' he said gravely, 'you could have included Bernadette, Anne, Pauline, Miriam, Clare— oh, and Frances—let's not forget Frances.'

'Oh, by all means let's not forget Frances,' Jodi snapped savagely. 'And now I'm going to my own room, and you won't stop me.'

'Oh? You're very sure of that, are you?' Those mesmeric eyes of his were on her face.

'Yes—and if you try to stop me, I'll rouse the whole household.' She stalked towards the door and with her hand on the doorknob turned to issue her parting shot, 'You . . . you . . . Bluebeard!'

But the exit line was wasted, for the knob would not turn under her hand. The door was locked. Panic swamped her, but she mustered enough courage to turn on him. 'Unlock this door—right now!'

'No,' he said calmly. He was beginning to move towards her, but Jodi evaded him, making for the door which he alleged led to his bedroom. She would make her escape that way.

As she flung open the door she heard him chuckle devilishly once more, and once inside the room she paused, confounded, for there was no other way out. The bedroom led off the drawing-room, but it was a dead end.

'I told you these were my quarters,' Griff drawled lazily from the doorway, 'fully self-contained. The only entry is through the door we came in by. And,' he added as she parted her lips, 'I wouldn't get any ideas about rousing the household. For one thing, we're a long way from the main part of the house, and, for another, these walls are very thick.' Smugly, 'My ancestors built well.'

'And were they a disreputable lot—like you?' she flung at him.

'By no means. Our family has always been very respectable.'

'Pity you had to go and ruin the tradition.'

He moved so swiftly that there was no time to anticipate his intentions. She was in his arms, her mouth silenced by a bruising kiss. For a moment she struggled impotently, but he only tightened his grip, rendering her incapable of movement. She tried to stay passive in his arms, but as always it was useless, and as she surrendered his kiss became sensual, his mouth softening, his tongue probing the soft inner lining of hers.

As always the taste, the touch, the scent of him proved too much for Jodi's defences. The blood leapt in her veins, her mouth opening, her head swimming as his hands slid down scorchingly over her body, drawing it closer to his. At once she was alive, wanting, needing ...

But with jarring suddenness, he released her. 'That,' he said huskily, 'still seems to be the only way to deal with your doubts of me. More effective than simple reasoning. But, for your information, my "bad reputation" comes—as I've pointed out before—from your highly over-developed imagination, and your suspicious nature. You, my dear Jodi, have put two and two together and come up—not with five as most people do, but with at least a dozen.'

Jodi was still reeling from his kiss. She took several unsteady backward steps, putting a very necessary distance between them. 'Yes,' she managed to say, 'a dozen women!'

He looked at her quizzically. 'Have you never trusted anyone, Jodi?'

'Yes, twice—and both times I've been let down.' Her pretty mouth twisted in distaste. 'First there was my father, whom I adored and looked up to. But he played away. Then there was Rodney——'

'Your father—and Rodney.' A lazy lifting of one dark brow. 'Is that all?' he drawled. 'Two men. Not a very high percentage on which to base your mistrust of the male sex.'

'The odds have risen since I met you,' she rejoined smartly.

He shook his head. 'No, you just think they have.'

'All right!' she taunted. 'Since you've got me trapped here, put your time to good use. Convince me.'

'I thought I'd already done that—last night.' There was a husky, seductive note in his voice. 'That I'd proved to you how I felt about you.'

A sense of weakness assailed her, but she fought against it. 'I...I didn't mean that. I meant—explain—about Victoria, Denise...and Co.'

Griff shook his head consideringly. 'I'd much rather you trusted me, believed that there's no one else in my life but you.'

'Sorry. All the evidence is against you.'

'You're going to feel pretty foolish,' he warned.

'I'd rather feel foolish than betrayed.'

He dismissed her claim with a shrug. 'Very well, if that's the way you want it.' He went over to a rosewood bureau that stood in a corner of the bedroom, and as he opened the top drawer and rifled through the contents Jodi glanced restlessly around her, still half hoping that there was some undiscovered means of escape.

It was a very masculine room, the décor in browns and rusts—just how she would have imagined Griff's room, in fact, furnished with taste but also for comfort. Deep armchairs either side of a fireplace which was obviously not just for show. Bookcases which showed him to be a prolific reader with a wide taste in literature. And the bed—an enormous bed, larger even than the one she had occupied last night, the bed she should be occupying right now. There was nothing in the room, as far as she could see, to serve as a reminder of his wife.

'Come here,' Griff commanded.

Nervously she moved towards him, alert for any attempt on his part to touch her. But instead he held out a large leather-bound photograph album, and wonderingly she took it, opened it and began to leaf through its pages.

There were photographs that obviously dated back for years, for some of them were becoming yellow and discoloured. Photographs of individuals—women and men, photographs of groups, of children—all neatly labelled. Jodi's mouth tightened as she continued her perusal. Finally she snapped the book shut and thrust it back at him, turned on her heel and marched towards the door. In the drawing-room at least she would be on more neutral ground.

The bedroom door resisted her efforts. Somehow he had found occasion to lock that too.

White-faced, taut-lipped, she turned on him. 'Let me out!' she demanded.

Lazily Griff shook his head, amusement in his eyes as he surveyed her indignant face. 'Not until you apologise.'

'I'm not going to apologise,' she declared defiantly. 'It's not my fault if you deliberately led me on, misled me. You let me go on making a fool of myself, didn't you—when a simple explanation——'

'This is the first time you've asked for an explanation,' he reminded her. 'If you'd had the sense to do so before, you wouldn't have built this up out of all proportion.'

That might seem the logical behaviour to him, but somehow she hadn't been able to... It had been as much a matter of pride as anything. She would not beg... She tried to impose some order on her swirling thoughts. 'You could have told me, when I took those messages for you, that Victoria, Denise, Sonia and Hilary were your sisters.'

He shook his head. 'Wrong again. Victoria, Denise, Sonia and *Bernadette* are my sisters.'

He was playing with her, making her work for the information. Jodi felt anger swelling inside her. Not just at him, but at her own vulnerability. 'Then who the hell is Hilary?'

'My brother.' And as she stared blankly, 'Didn't you know Hilary was a man's name as well as a woman's?'

She did, of course. But the thought had simply never occurred to her.

'And for your information—before any more telephone calls give you the wrong idea—my other brother is called Vyvian.'

She had to ask, 'And the other names you mentioned—Anne, Pauline... I can't remember all of them.'

'Miriam, Clare and Frances? They're all my nieces—Frances was born just last week. I once told you, remember, that I had no nephews.' He regarded her calmly, waiting, one eyebrow half cocked, humorous, quizzical.

And Jodi's own sense of humour, badly swamped of late by other more painful emotions, rose to the surface. First a reluctant smile, then a giggle escaped her. 'You swine!' she said, but it was a laughing, affectionate accusation.

'And now,' Griff said, 'do you think we could adjourn this hearing and get back to the matter in hand?'

'What matter?' she queried.

'Us. You and me,' his eyes darkened, 'and that very comfortable bed over there.' His hands clamped down on her shoulders, hard fingers almost bruising in their intensity as he drew her to him, her lips meeting his with an inevitability as natural as breathing, and searing waves of desire swept through her.

She clung to him, her hands tangling in his hair, her body revelling in the pressure of his. At first she was unaware of the fact that he was drawing her towards the bed and then he was lowering her gently on to it.

'No!' Jodi struggled up, hands pushing him away.

'Now what?' he demanded exasperatedly as she shook her head.

'This isn't right, Griff. Oh, I know I...I didn't stick to my convictions last night. You . . . you have this uncanny ability to overcome my better judgement. But I meant what I said about... about being under your parents' roof. I——'

'Jodi, to all intents and purposes you're under *my* roof. I told you, remember, this wing is mine. Ever since I reached my majority it's been an accepted fact that what I do here, who I bring here, is my business. And before you can get back on your high horse and ask me who else I've brought here, the answer is just one person—my late wife.'

Without waiting for her reply, he caught her to him again, trailing burning kisses along the line of her throat, and excitement flickered through her. When she was with Griff like this she seemed to have no will of her own. It was not something to which she was accustomed. Apart from Rodney, her few brief relationships had never moved beyond friendship. She realised she had never really assessed a man physically before. But Griff was a magnificent specimen, his body—clothed or unclothed—had an incredible effect on her. Never in her life had she been so devastatingly affected as she was by Griff.

'Jodi?' He held her away a little, looking down into her face. 'How soon can we be married?'

'What?' She couldn't believe what she'd just heard. Words she had never expected to hear. 'What did you say?'

He smiled down at her. 'Lovemaking afflicts me with deafness too—at least, making love to you does. I said, when can we be married? How soon?' And as she still gazed dumbfounded at him, 'Now what's wrong?'

'We...you... Nothing was ever said about...about marriage.'

'What?' The eyes which had been languorously warm before were now chips of ice. 'What are you trying to say, Jodi?'

'When we were at the hospital——'

'When we were at the hospital, you were worried out of your mind. And I agreed to wait until a more suitable place and time to discuss things.'

'But I thought——'

His face seemed strained and drawn now, harsh lines etched around his nose and mouth. 'You thought, quite obviously, that I was the kind of man who slept around. I don't, Jodi. I've only been to bed with two women, and both of them were the women I intended to marry. It's always been my intention to marry you, from the first moment I set eyes on you.'

'But——'

'Obviously I couldn't say anything at first. You made it all too clear you wouldn't be easy to persuade. But I was determined to persuade you. And if marriage wasn't what you had in mind, then you're not what I took you for. Oh,' he added bitterly, 'I'll still go on loving you, wanting you. But I warn you, with me it's marriage or nothing, Jodi. I——'

'Griff, do shut up!' And as his face darkened ominously, 'Just let me get a word in edgeways, will you? You've got it all wrong. I thought *you* didn't want marriage. You've only ever talked about "wanting"— about where were we going to live. Is it any wonder I thought——?'

His expression lightened. 'Does that mean——?'

'It means,' Jodi said softly, 'that I wouldn't settle for anything less than marriage either.'

She had confidently expected that, on hearing this assertion, he would pull her into his arms again and that things would take their natural course. But he was studying her reflectively, a puzzled frown creasing his brow.

'If that's so... and you thought all I wanted was... why did you——?'

'Why did I let you make love to me—twice? I know,' she flushed painfully. 'It must sound illogical. But... but love *is* an illogical emotion. Whenever you're near me, Griff, whatever else my brain is telling me just seems to be swamped.' She moved towards him, set her hand on his arm, looked up at him pleadingly. 'I love you, Griff, and I'll marry you whenever you like. Although...'

He tensed. 'Although what?'

'I would like to wait until Sally is well enough.'

He relaxed. 'Of course, you goose. And now,' he eyed her speculatively, 'are you still set on going to your own bed? Are you going to insist on our waiting now until——'

Laughingly, Jodi set a hand over his lips, 'No,' she said softly, 'I'm not going to insist.'

'Jodi? Would you like breakfast in bed? Jodi?'

'Hmm?' Reluctantly, Jodi's eyes opened. She had been dreaming—of her wedding day. She was just gliding down the aisle of a picturesque old country church on her brother-in-law's arm, Sally following as matron of honour, and she hadn't wanted to wake up.

'I said,' Griff repeated patiently, 'would you like breakfast in bed?'

'No...oh, is it that time?' She jerked upright. 'Heavens! Robin and Tanya...their breakfast...'

'Relax,' he pulled her back, 'Molly is seeing to all that.'

'But she shouldn't have to. It's my responsibility...' She broke off, then, 'How did she know——?' she began accusingly.

'I rang down to the kitchen, of course,' he indicated the bedside phone. 'The same way I'll order breakfast if you want it.'

Jodi shook her head. 'No, thanks.' She didn't want the Griffithses' staff to see her established in Griff's bed, not until their plans had been officially announced. 'I must get back to my own room and have a shower and get dressed.'

'You could shower here,' Griff suggested, and then, with wicked innuendo, 'we both could.'

The idea was tempting, achingly so, but again she shook her head. 'I need clean clothes.' She slid her legs over the side of the vast bed. 'I must go.' And protestingly, 'Griff!' as a long determined arm snaked about her waist, holding her back.

'You don't think I'm going to let you go without my good morning kiss?'

'Of course not—I'm sorry.' Unsuspectingly, she turned towards him, only to find that he had far more in mind than the chaste salute she had expected. 'Griff!' she protested again, and then, weakly, 'Oh, Griff!'

A good hour later as, finally, she showered and shampooed her silky hair, Jodi had leisure to wonder how Griff's family would receive the news of their engagement. If he was to be believed, he had already hinted at his plans, and today would only be the confirmation. Nevertheless, she felt exceedingly nervous as she took a last look in the mirror, smoothing down the green woollen dress she had chosen to wear today.

It was something of an anticlimax to come downstairs and to find that her host and hostess were out.

'They've gone for pre-lunch drinks with some old friends of theirs—in the next village,' Griff said almost absently, his eyes caressing Jodi as she stood before him, the simple lines of the dress emphasising her wandlike slimness, a slimness that contrasted strongly with the full high breasts, the upper curves of which just appeared in the V-shaped neckline.

'Did you ... did you say anything to them, about ... about——?'

'They'd already left by the time I came down. Look, it's too late for breakfast now. Why don't we have brunch instead and then make an early start for London?'

'The children——' Jodi began.

'The children will be quite happy with Mrs Monkton.'

'But I promised Sally——'

'Tomorrow, hmm? Today I want you all to myself.' And she couldn't argue with that.

It was a happy sight that greeted them when they entered the maternity ward.

'Barry!' Jodi exclaimed. 'You managed to get here!'

Her brother-in-law was seated on the side of the bed, one arm around his wife, the other nursing his infant son. And Sally turned a glowing face to her sister.

'Isn't it marvellous, Jodi? Barry's been able to swing a month's leave—not just two weeks—on compassionate grounds. He says he'll look after the children, so we won't be keeping you from your work any more.'

'Are you sure?' Jodi had enjoyed looking after her niece and nephew—though of late, she thought guiltily, she'd had plenty of help in that direction—but it would be a relief to be able to go in and check up on things at her boutique. Though whether it would be her boutique for much longer was a debatable point.

'Quite sure. I'll pick them up later this afternoon,' Barry told her.

'I'll ring home and tell them to expect you,' Griff promised. 'Otherwise they might suspect you of kidnapping!'

They did not linger long at the hospital after that, since Jodi felt sure Sally would rather have her husband's uninterrupted company.

'We don't have to go home yet,' said Griff as they got back into the car.

Home? Jodi supposed the Kentish house would be home to her one day. But she wasn't sure she wanted to begin her married life under his parents' roof.

'What do you suggest, then?' she asked.

He shot his cuff to look at his wristwatch, and just the sight of the soft hairs banding his arm made Jodi's stomach somersault crazily. Unable to restrain herself, she reached out and tentatively fingered it.

His eyes darkened and smouldered as he turned to look at her. 'It's several hours since we made love,' he said huskily. 'I'm not sure I can wait until we get home—and I suspect you feel the same way?'

Jodi dipped her head, feeling the betraying colour rising in her cheeks, her body throbbing its own telltale message. She cleared her throat, suddenly strangely obstructed. 'We...we could go to my flat, I suppose,' she murmured.

'Or mine.'

Her head shot up again. 'You have a flat? You've never mentioned it.'

'Because on the occasions when it would have been appropriate, the Hampstead house has been nearer.' His hand covered her knee, exerting a warm, exciting pressure. 'As I said, I find it very difficult to wait where you're concerned.'

She swallowed again. 'And...and we're not far from your flat now?'

'Five minutes.' He looked at her questioningly.

'I...I'd like to see where you live,' she said shyly.

'Is that all?' he teased. 'Just curiosity?'

Again that painful blush. 'You...you know it's not.'

He accelerated out of the car park, whisking around side streets, empty with the Boxing Day hush. As he had predicted, it took precisely five minutes, and then they were drawing up in a picturesque little mews. Each house in the row was painted pristine white against which the windowboxes, empty now, stood out in a bright vibrant blue. The door to which he led her was adorned by a gleaming brass knocker.

'When you said "flat", I imagined an enormous block,' she confessed.

He shook his head, 'I like a bit more character in my home than that.'

'I suppose it would seem a bit soulless after your parents' house,' she agreed. Then, 'Griff...' She hesitated, not quite sure how to put it and if she dared... and then, encouraged by his questioning smile, 'Where would we live when... if...'

'*When* is the word you want,' he said firmly. 'Let's not be in any doubt about that. We *are* going to be married as soon as is humanly possible. I intend to make sure of you before you can slip through my fingers on some ridiculous quibble. *When* we get married, we shall live here—to begin with.'

'And then?' she asked, as he ushered her through the front door into a diminutive hallway.

'And then I thought we might go house-hunting. This place,' as he led her into the one downstairs room, 'is only a bachelor flat. Once the children start arriving...' He laughed delightedly. 'You blush exquisitely, Jodi. But,' anxiously, 'you do agree? There *are* going to be children?'

She nodded and then, mischievously, as he swung her up into his arms and made for the staircase that spiralled up to the floor above, 'For all you know— the way you've been behaving lately—they might already be on the way.'

Griff stopped halfway up the stairs, and Jodi would have laughed if she had not found his expression so touching. It must be the first time in their acquaintance that she had known Griff at a loss for words.

'You mean you could be... You don't.... I mean...the Pill?'

'There's never been any need for that sort of precaution,' she reminded him simply, and felt his arms tighten.

'I know. Oh, Jodi,' he muttered huskily against her neck, 'I'm so glad, so unutterably glad that I was the first with you. But,' as he carried her into the one large bedroom, 'you didn't say...could you be...are you——?'

'I don't know—yet,' she admitted.

His fingers were at the front buttoning of the demure wool dress, which fell softly about her feet, leaving only delicate underthings to bar his seeking hands and lips. 'And would you mind—if you were?'

'Not a bit,' she said softly against his mouth.

'In that case,' he was rapidly divesting himself of his clothing, 'it won't hurt to make sure...'

Jodi laughed delightedly as she welcomed him into her arms. 'As if you needed any excuse,' she teased lovingly.

It was dark when they drove back into the Kentish countryside, Jodi's head drooping sleepily against Griff's shoulder. It would be wonderful, she mused, when they were together for all time, with no need for partings. How pleased Sally would be—and triumphant—when she told her the news. 'A man for

Christmas' had been Sally's dearest wish for her—and almost miraculously that wish had come true.

They were just in time for the evening meal. Mrs Griffiths met them with the news that Barry had collected the children as promised.

'A pity really,' she said wistfully. 'They were here for such a short time.'

'Never mind, Mother,' Griff said bracingly, 'you've a beautiful clutch of grandchildren——'

'But no little boys. Robin was rather a darling.'

'Well,' Griff drawled. 'I can't make any promises, of course, but you never know, Jodi and I may be able to change that.'

His mother's head shot up sharply. 'You mean you've finally asked her?' and as Griff nodded, 'Oh, my dear,' she came towards Jodi, 'I'm so pleased. David said he hadn't asked you yet and that we weren't to come the heavy prospective in-laws in case we frightened you off... But now...' she kissed Jodi's cheek warmly, and Jodi recognised that under the apparently cool exterior Mrs Griffiths had been hiding an anxiety almost as great as Griff's own. 'It's been my dearest wish for David to find happiness again. I was so afraid he'd remain immured in that bachelor pad of his for the rest of his days.'

'I don't think there was much fear of that,' Jodi couldn't help saying with a teasing smile at Griff. 'Not all women are as slow at recognising worth as I am.'

Her reward was the dark loving glow in his eyes that promised deeper, more fruitful recompense to follow.

Later that evening, when once more they were alone together, she asked him, a trifle anxiously, if he would have any objection to her carrying on with her work, 'Until we start a family? Of course, once we had a baby I'd stay at home and be a proper mother to it. But I could retain an interest in the boutique, couldn't I?'

'If that's what you want. No one could ever accuse me of being old-fashioned. And I've never been a great believer in the concept that woman's place is entirely in the home. June went on working after we were married, and of course there were never any children before... before she...'

'I know,' Jodi whispered comfortingly, winding her arms about his neck. 'And now,' she said, after he had kissed her very satisfactorily, '*I am* going to be very old-fashioned and insist on sleeping in my own bed tonight. Yes,' softly as he made to protest, 'I know it's the wrong way round, but from now on I want an old-fashioned romantic courtship. Otherwise,' demurely, bouncing to her feet, 'what will I have to look forward to on my wedding night?'

He growled menacingly. 'I'll show you what you have to look forward to,' he threatened, but laughingly she shook her head, escaping his reaching arms.

For a long, long moment his eyes compelled hers, almost but not quite succeeding in weakening her resolve. Then, 'Oh, I suppose I must let you have your own way. But I can see how it's going to be,' he grumbled humorously. 'The rest of my life is going to be spent inextricably wound around your little finger.'

As she made her way to her own room, Jodi felt a little twinge of regret at her decision and that Griff had accepted it quite so readily. But it was the right thing to do, she assured herself. They knew of their love for each other now, but for a marriage to succeed it must keep its freshness, its excitement. By retaining a little of her mystery, by being occasionally unpredictable, she would always ensure his interest, his determined pursuit.

She fell asleep with a satisfied little smile on her lips.

CHAPTER EIGHT

JODI'S alarm clock rang early on the Tuesday morning after Christmas. Usually she was a reluctant riser, so this morning at first, when she woke, she couldn't think where she was and what had prompted the warm glow of wellbeing she felt.

Then she remembered, and leapt joyfully out of bed. True, she was back in her own flat, not living in proximity to Griff any more. Outside it was a dismal grey, rain-filled day. It might be a workaday morning; she might have planned to go in today and try to find out what future, if any, the boutique had.

But aside from that little cloud on the horizon, everything was as right with her world as if there were blazing sunshine in the London streets. She was going to marry Griff in three weeks' time, and far from disapproving of her, as she had feared, his parents were delighted. And Griff was looking forward to introducing her to the rest of his family.

'New Year's Eve will be a good opportunity,' he'd said. 'We're planning a surprise party—hence all the family phone calls.'

'Surprise party? For whom?' she asked.

'My mother. New Year's Eve is also her sixtieth birthday.'

It was the postman's arrival, while she was having her breakfast, which reminded Jodi of the still unopened mail in her handbag. Today's crop of envelopes only yielded up cards that had arrived too late for

Christmas. She fetched her handbag and ripped the envelopes open to study their contents while she drank her coffee.

As she had suspected, for the most part they were bills and bank statements, but one envelope she had overlooked before puzzled her, long, thick and embossed with the name of a firm she didn't recognise.

Inside, however, the headed notepaper cleared up the mystery—a firm of solicitors.

At first she couldn't understand what she was reading. She read it again with mounting bewilderment and disbelief. It couldn't be true. He couldn't do this to her—he wouldn't! Her thoughts whirled chaotically—doubt, anger and finally a sense of anguished betrayal succeeding each other. The devious, cheating ... The letter read:

> We are now empowered to reveal the name of our clients purchasing the property of which your premises form part. Messrs Griffiths Brothers have asked us to contact you on their behalf and to advise you that, regretfully, they are unable to extend your lease. Please be good enough to contact our office at your earliest convenience.

Furiously, Jodi crumpled the paper into a ball and thrust it from her, her eyes closed in a vain attempt to shut out the pain of this revelation. But it was useless. Griff...Griff of all people was the one buying up Goodbody's Store and putting an end to the little business she had worked so hard to build up. For she knew she would never be able to find—or afford to rent—premises so central again. Since the boutique had opened, rentals in the area had soared.

Oh, no wonder he'd been so smugly complacent about her carrying on with her work, when he knew damned well she wouldn't be able to.

'And all this while,' she muttered savagely, 'he's known how worried I was about the boutique, but he's never said a word.' And so great was her anger at this silent deception, it did not occur to her that the circumstances were rather different. 'The swindler! It's Rodney all over again.'

Leaving her coffee untasted, she flung on her coat and hurried out of the flat. She would go and see his solicitors all right. And then she would go and see Griff himself. She would tell him just what she thought of his underhand machinations.

The morning which had started so well went from bad to worse. As well as the rain a strong wind blew. Jodi's umbrella turned inside out, she stepped unwarily into a puddle, and to cap it all, when she arrived at the solicitors' office they were still closed for their Christmas break. Jodi rarely if ever used bad language, but this was the last straw, and she swore feelingly.

Afterwards she thought that, had she been able to confront the solicitors, it might have defused some of her anger. As it was, she set off again, for the boutique this time, still at boiling point. And discussing the situation with her two assistants only added to her simmering rage, for the closure of the shop would also put them out of work, and since one girl was a one-parent family with two children to support...

She declined to stay and have coffee with them.

'I've been rehearsing all the way here what I'm going to say to the man responsible for this, and the sooner I see him the better,' she decided.

Griffiths Brothers' store was quiet on this first post-holiday morning of trading. Their New Year sales did not start until the end of the week. Jodi marched militantly across the almost deserted ground floor and into the lift which would take her up to the office level.

On this floor everything screamed wealth and luxury. 'Money gained by treading on the face of the small shopkeeper,' she muttered to herself, and made a mental note to include that remark in her planned diatribe.

She knocked peremptorily on the outer door of the office suite and without waiting for an answer flung the door open and walked in.

A surprised secretary confronted her—a stranger, not Mrs Monkton as she had half expected and feared.

'Can I help you?'

'I want to see Mr Griffiths,' Jodi said tautly.

'Have you an appointment?'

'No.' Frustration boiled up inside Jodi, but it wasn't this girl's fault that she worked for an unprincipled toad. 'But I think you'll find he'll see me.'

She couldn't even use the lever that she was his fiancée, she thought grimly, because, by the time she had finished what she wanted to say, she wouldn't be. Hers must be the shortest engagement on record. She might even qualify for the Guinness Book of Records—such inconsequential thoughts flashed through her vexed mind.

'Could I have your name?' Still looking doubtful, the girl depressed a button on her desk. 'There's a Miss Knight here to see you, sir.' There was a deep rumble of reply, then to Jodi, 'All right, you can go in.' She indicated the inner door.

Jodi swept in, and before she could lose her courage rushed into her condemnatory speech, addressing herself to the back view silhouetted against the window. But she was only a few words into her prepared accusation—words that mainly concerned her opinion of Griff's character—when the man turned, and her voice trailed away in puzzled confusion as she found herself confronting a complete stranger.

No, not a complete stranger—for he bore a certain resemblance to Griff which proclaimed him a member of the same family. Certainly from the back view she had taken him for Griff. But there were differences. This man was younger and his features were less strongly defined.

'I . . . I'm sorry,' Jodi faltered. 'I . . . I thought you were Griff.'

His face cleared. 'Ah, I wondered what *I* had done to deserve such opprobrium. Well, I'm afraid my brother isn't here. Can I——?'

'Where is he?' Jodi demanded.

'He's been called away unexpectedly—on business, at one of our other branches. Can I be of any help?'

Jodi shook her head. 'No, what I want to say has to be said to Griff.'

'Are you by any chance the Miss Knight, the Jodi he——?'

'Yes.' But Jodi didn't want to go into that. 'When will he be back?'

'I can't say definitely. Can I get him to contact you?'

Jodi wavered. If Griff had been here this morning there would have been no stopping her. By now he would have known exactly what she thought of him. But this setback in her plans had destroyed all her impetus. She was still angry, furiously angry, but now she also felt increasingly depressed. Perhaps it would be better if she just didn't see Griff again.

'Don't bother,' she said at last.

She turned on her heel and left the office and the building more slowly than she had entered. She felt suddenly, ineffably weary. Until recently she had always prided herself on her independence of spirit. Now she realised just how much she had come to depend on Griff. And with the discovery of his treachery she felt as though one of the mainstays of her life had been suddenly wrenched away, leaving her off balance and uncertain.

Griff had been so marvellous when she was worried about Sally and she had needed to talk to someone. Now, once again, she badly needed a confidant, but she could not turn to him this time.

Nor could she go bothering Sally. Her sister was still in hospital, still regaining her own strength.

But she could go home—to her mother, she thought suddenly.

After her parents' divorce, her mother had stayed on in the family home. Both Jodi and Sally tried to visit her as often as possible, and, although she had built a new life for herself, she was always delighted to see her daughters, but she lived too far away for regular weekend visits.

Sally and Jodi had always tried not to take sides in their parents' disagreements. They loved both of them equally. But now Jodi found herself beginning to sympathise with her mother. She too had been betrayed by a man. She of all people would understand.

Back at her flat, Jodi hurriedly piled clothes into a large suitcase, sufficient for a long stay. As she did so she felt slightly ashamed of her own cowardice. She had never run away from anything before in her life—not even after the rift with Rodney. But she was running away from Griff.

It wasn't far to seek to find out why. Now that her first violent anger had abated, she was afraid that if she saw him the strong sexual attraction between them would make it impossible for her to sustain her righteous indignation. She knew only too well how traitorously her flesh could behave where he was concerned. And he had probably counted on that in his dealings with her.

Just as she was about to leave the flat the telephone rang. For a moment she hesitated, all her instincts telling her to walk away and ignore it. But she never had been able to ignore a telephone. And it might not be him. She lifted the receiver.

'Hallo?' It was Griff's familiar, heart-shaking voice, sounding blurred and a long way off. 'Jodi? I'm calling from Bristol. My brother rang me. He said you——'

She slammed the receiver down and then, before he could re-establish contact and she could weaken, she fled, banging the front door behind her.

For the first time since she'd been living in London, she wished she owned her own car. At Sally's she'd had the use of her sister's vehicle to run Robin to nursery and for shopping errands. Now, her heavy suitcase bumping at her shins, she had to wait several minutes for a taxi.

It was ridiculous—Griff was far away in Bristol, several hours' journey, she told herself, but she still felt this quivering anxiety to be gone before he could catch up with her.

With a sigh of relief she sank into the taxi and directed the driver to take her to Euston. Griff was in the south-west. She was going north-west. But geographically she could be no further away from him than she felt now, mentally and physically, and as she boarded the train she had to fight back the silly weak tears that pricked at her eyes.

'Darling, how lovely to see you!'

Her mother's welcome at her Blackpool home was all that Jodi could have hoped for. She only wished she were visiting her under happier circumstances. But to Jodi's chagrin, her reason for the visit did not receive quite as sympathetic a hearing.

'Perhaps you were unwise to leave London without seeing him. Maybe you should have given him a chance to explain. It's taken me years to realise it,' her mother confessed, 'but if I'd asked your father more questions instead of just hurling accusations at him, our marriage might never have foundered. I sometimes think my intolerance of his business trips, my jealousy actually drove him into other women's arms.' A comment which left Jodi with much uncomfortable food for thought. Had she not been guilty of that very thing when she had suspected Griff of having a multiplicity of affairs?

Then she hardened her heart again. That had been an entirely different matter. There was no way he could have explained away his deceit about the purchase of Goodbody's and the cessation of her lease.

Her mother was right about one thing, though; she should have had the courage of her earlier convictions and stayed in London to confront him. She realised now that she hadn't been thinking clearly. She should have fought harder to save her business, for the renewal of her lease. But now she was here she might as well stay for a few days and think things over, plan her strategy.

Despite the wintry conditions, the sea air was a bracing change from city dust and traffic fumes.

Blackpool, out of season, was a quiet, almost desolate place, with closed cafés, boarded-up amusement arcades.

To assist her thinking processes, and well wrapped up, Jodi took long walks along the beach at low tide, turning her face up to the sea breezes, drinking in the scent of ozone, attaining some measure of peace. But despite the unaccustomed fresh air and exercise, her normally healthy appetite seemed to have disappeared. Somehow food seemed to stick in her throat— and then there was the nausea, especially early in the morning.

By the end of those few days and despite all her deliberations, she was certain of only one thing. She was pregnant.

Jodi took a long hard look at her future. Her first reaction had been one of euphoria. She was carrying Griff's child, something she had dreamed of. But she soon came down to earth. The circumstances were totally different now. And the very fact of her pregnancy made a difference to her plans.

She couldn't go back and face Griff now, aware as she was of the new life within her. In one of the moments of weakness that inevitably seemed to assail her in his presence, she might reveal her secret. And then it would look as though she had gone meekly back, prepared to overlook his deceit, for the sake of having a father for her baby.

She told her mother that she was pregnant, and her mother was horrified. She came of a generation when being an unmarried mother carried the stigma of social disgrace.

'Whatever will you do?' she wanted to know.

'I shall have the baby, of course.' To Jodi anything else was inconceivable. She had been surprised to find that the growing life within her was so immediately, so compellingly real.

'Of course. I didn't mean ... But you'll give it up for adoption?' her mother suggested.

'No way!' Jodi exploded. 'There's no way I'm going through nine months of pregnancy just to meekly hand my child over to someone else's care!'

'Then you'll have to tell——'

'Let's get one thing straight, Mum. I am not telling Griff. I'll give up the London flat, get a job up here somewhere. Things are cheaper here than in London. I'll manage.'

It was easy to say, but far harder to do when all her instincts screamed that Griff had a moral right to know about his child. But it was easy to argue that *she'd* had a right to know about the fate of her boutique. He had kept secrets from her; now she would keep one from him.

Another week passed, during which she wrote to the estate agents through whom she rented her flat, terminating the lease. She also wrote to the boutique, informing her assistants of her decision not to fight Griffiths Brothers and wishing them luck with future employment. 'If you could pack up any remaining stock and take it to my sister's house, I'd be very grateful,' she told them.

The letter to Sally was more difficult, but in the end she merely told her sister that she had broken with Griff and that she was tired of city life, that she had decided, for the future, to make her home in the north-west, 'To be near Mum.'

'Sally won't believe a word of it—she knows you too well. She'll be on the phone the minute she gets your letter,' her mother warned.

Jodi shrugged. 'It won't make any difference. And whatever you do, don't tell her I'm pregnant. I shan't.'

Returning from one of her long walks just in time for their evening meal, Jodi met her mother, on the doorstep, wearing her hat and coat and obviously about to leave the house.

'Where on earth are you going at this time of day, Mum?' she asked. Usually her mother was to be found in the kitchen, preparing some succulent dish to tempt her daughter's poor appetite.

'I...oh, just popping out...something I forgot...'

'Can't I go for you?' Jodi was puzzled by her mother's almost furtive manner. She was acting very strangely—almost as if she were guilty of some misdemeanour.

'No...no, I'd rather go myself. I could do with some fresh air. You...you go in and lay the table for me.' And with that her mother scuttled away as if afraid Jodi would either detain or follow her.

Very suspicious. And very uncharacteristic. Could her mother possibly have a date? an amused Jodi wondered. In the two weeks she'd been at home her mother had gone out very little without her, and there hadn't been any mention of a man friend, only bridge-playing women friends. Oh, well, no doubt she would find out what it was all about when her mother returned. She opened the front door.

The usual appetising smells wafted into the little hallway from the kitchen. Jodi flung her coat and woollen hat on to the newel-post at the foot of the stairs and went to investigate. She stopped on the kitchen threshold, clutching at the doorpost for support as the room seemed suddenly to tilt and spin around her.

'Jodi? Jodi, are you all right?'

It was Griff coming towards her, his rugged face concerned, hands outstretched. But it couldn't be Griff, she thought giddily. He didn't know where she was. Then she remembered her mother's guilty expression and a groan escaped her. She might have known. With a superhuman effort she was in control again. She backed away from the outstretched hands.

'Leave me alone. I'm OK,' she croaked, and then, more strongly, 'What are *you* doing here?'

'Stirring the pot,' Griff said. 'Your mother said she'd be half an hour.' He gestured towards the stove, where a large saucepan steamed fragrantly. And for the first time Jodi noticed that he wore one of her mother's aprons around his waist—and that the totally feminine garment did not detract one iota from his masculinity, the effects of which were already having their fatal effect upon her. She wasn't sure she could cope with this.

'I meant,' she said savagely, 'what are you doing in Blackpool—in my mother's house? Oh, just wait till she comes back! How dare she go behind my back and——'

'Your mother had no idea I was coming, until I turned up on the doorstep. And I should have thought it was obvious why I'm here.' He removed the apron and flung it on to the back of a chair. 'I've come to see you. I want to know——'

'Well, I don't want to see you—ever,' Jodi said. But she found it hard to sound convincing even to herself. Just the sight of him was destroying all her resolve. She wanted nothing more than to be able to throw herself into his arms, to tell him how much she loved him, to tell him moreover that she carried the proof of that love. But he didn't deserve her love, he didn't deserve to know. He was a deceitful, cheating, conniving...

'Shall we go and sit down?' Griff suggested. 'We have to talk.' Despite her immediate protest he took hold of her arm and propelled her towards the living-room. 'You look tired.' The concern in his voice made her eyes smart.

She tried to shake free of him. 'I don't want to talk to you. We've nothing to talk about.'

'Oh, but I think we have. I don't know what crime I'm supposed to have committed this time. All my brother——'

'If you'd been in your office that day, instead of your brother, yes, I would have had plenty to say to you. But now...' Jodi shrugged. 'I can't be bothered. It just isn't worth it.' She averted her face. 'Please go now, Griff.' Go now, she added to herself, before I disgrace myself by bursting into tears because I've so longed for the sight and sound of you, the touch and the scent of you.

'We're going to talk!' he said grimly. He pushed her down on to a settee and sat beside her, his hand still on her arm, preventing her from jumping up again. 'All my brother was able to relate was the string of epithets you applied to me. When I telephoned your flat you slammed the receiver down on me. And when I got back to London you'd disappeared.'

She was still looking anywhere but at him. It was impossible to face him without letting her conflicting feelings show. 'Then how did you find me, if Mum didn't——?'

'It wasn't easy,' Griff said grimly. 'I didn't like to bother your sister at first——'

'At first?' Now Jodi did turn towards him. 'But you did ask Sally?' she accused indignantly. 'And she told you? Oh, how could she, after I expressly forbade——'

'She took a lot of persuading. But once I'd convinced her that it *was* in your best interests to see me——'

'In my best interests!' Jodi echoed scornfully. 'It seems to me my best interests are the last thing you've had at heart. Oh, it's a pity I didn't tell Sally just what sort of a man you are, David Griffiths. And how dare you go bothering her, when you know how ill she's been, when she's only just come out of hospital——'

'I told you, I didn't go bothering her—not at first. It was a last resort. I tried the boutique first. But I didn't find the girls there very sympathetic—they either couldn't, or wouldn't——'

'Oh,' sarcastically, 'so you did know where to find the boutique, then?'

He raised a puzzled brow. 'Not initially, no. I had to make enquiries. Anyway, as I said, it did me no good. I——'

'Oh,' Jodi snorted rudely, 'come off it! If anyone knows where it is, you should. And to think I thought I'd finally met someone I could trust. Trust me, you said—and like a fool I did. And all the while, behind my back...' Her voice trailed away and she bit her lip in an effort to stop its quivering.

'Jodi!' Griff's hands were on her shoulders, firm but gentle. 'Suppose you stop talking in riddles and tell me what this is all about.'

'Stop pretending,' she said fiercely. 'You know damn well what you've done to me.'

He shook his head, his expression wry. 'So far as I'm aware my only offence has been to fall in love with you.'

Jodi bit her lip to stop its tendency to tremble. 'I might have believed that once. But now I know what your little scheme was. It was all a ploy——'

'In that case you know more than I do,' Griff said wryly. 'What *are* you getting at?'

'I'm talking about the fact that you've put me out of business——'

His grip tightened. '*I*'ve put *you* out of business? What the hell is this, Jodi? Talk plainly, damn you.'

Jodi looked at him in stunned disbelief. How could he be so hypocritical? How could he keep up the pretence?

'I don't *need* to tell you,' she said scornfully, 'but, since you insist on keeping up this charade, I will— if only to demonstrate to you that however naïve I may have been in the past, you can't deceive me any longer. As you very well know, my boutique was on part of Goodbodys' property. *You* are buying up Goodbody's and *you* are terminating my lease.'

He was actually shaking his head. 'Hold on a minute, I——'

'No,' she snapped, '*you* hold on. Hear me out. You've asked for it and you're going to get it all. You lied to me, Griff. You said I'd be able to go on working at the boutique after we were married. After we were married!' she repeated bitterly. 'And all the time you knew there wouldn't be any boutique. Is it any wonder I asked myself if there was really going to be any marriage? Did you really think I was so blindly infatuated with you that the business wouldn't matter to me? Is that why you——?'

'And did you really suppose,' he snapped, becoming angry in his turn, 'that with a firm as large as ours I'd need to go to such devious lengths to buy out a tinpot little boutique?' He stood up and moved away from her, hands thrust deeply into his trouser pockets as though to restrain himself from violence.

Jodi jumped up too. 'Tinpot!' she blazed at him. 'You condescending pig! I remember now, you patronised my boutique once before. Just because you were born into a rich family business——'

'Exactly the point I'm making.' Griff sounded exasperated. 'I don't *need* to put you out of business. No, Jodi,' as her lips parted, 'stop right there—' his eyes were green ice, 'before you say anything else you're going to regret later.'

'The only thing I regret,' she told him bitterly, 'is having met you in the first place. I——'

'That simply is not true, and you know it.' Two strides and he grasped her shoulders, pulled her closer and subjected her to one of his long intense gazes.

Jodi felt her heart turn over and her legs begin to shake, but she mustn't weaken. 'It *is* true. And it's not just me you've ruined. You're putting two other people out of work—one of whom can ill afford——'

'Jodi!' crisply he interrupted her. 'I've been very patient. I've listened to what you have to say. Now you're going to listen to me. You've been performing your usual mathematical impossibility—making two and two add up to some improbable answer.'

'No, I——'

'Yes, you have. Ever since the very first time we met you've misunderstood my every motive. Until now I've made allowances, knowing how you've been let down in the past. But enough is enough. This is the last time I'm going to vindicate myself. There *has* to be trust between husband and wife. When we're married——'

'We're not going to be——'

But her defiant words were cut off by the pressure of his mouth, uncompromisingly applied to hers.

She tried to resent what he was doing to her, the methods he was using to overcome her resistance. But a sudden upsurge of yearning swamped all the fight in her, leaving her weak and pliant. She felt Griff's chest rise and fall on a swift breath as he sensed the softening of her mouth, the tension ebbing from her body.

His voice was husky against her lips, 'God, Jodi, if you knew what these last two weeks have done to me.'

And to me, she thought hazily, her arms linked around his neck, her body curved to his, her lips parted to allow his exploring tongue full licence.

The hardness of his lips had altered to a kiss of warm sensuality, his hand sliding down her spine, holding her so that she was quiveringly aware of him, of his arousal.

'Jodi,' he groaned, 'I want you—God, how I want you. It's been too long. Far too long.' His breath was warm against her skin as his mouth slid down the column of her throat, his hand sliding up beneath her sweater to seek breasts that had already swollen and peaked with her desire. To know his caress again was exquisite pleasure, and the rest of her body ached enviously.

Her need to touch him in return was overwhelming, and she tugged at the buttons of his shirt, finding the warm roughness of his chest. She pressed closer to him. 'Griff, I——'

'No, Jodi, not yet. There's something we have to settle first.'

She gave a little mew of protest as he pulled away, released her and stepped back. A glance at his flushed face, the dilated pupils of his eyes, told her that he shared her need. So why. . . ?

'Now that I've proved to you—and to myself—that all this talk of not wanting to see me again is rubbish——'

'Oh!' Jodi gasped, humiliated. It was true. As usual his proximity had drained all the fight out of her.

'Now don't get on your high horse again,' he warned. 'Just listen. We have to clear the air. I won't make love to you with doubts still lying between us.' He put the width of the room between them, but his gaze never for one instant left her face. 'I think I know what's happened. I told you some while ago that my particular interest in Griffiths Brothers is the merchandise and public relations side. My brother Vyvian looks after the property angle.'

Jodi took a step towards him. 'Are you saying——?'

'Wait.' An upraised hand held her back. 'Let me finish. Vyvian and I do each other the courtesy of trusting each other to carry out our individual functions, and we have a meeting every two or three months to discuss recent developments. I was aware that Vyvian was in negotiation for some new premises. But...' He paused and went on with emphasis, 'I give you my word I had no idea which premises they were—or that your boutique formed part of them.'

She studied his face, desperately wanting to believe him, and deciding, as she met his direct steady gaze, that she did. She heaved a little sigh of relief.

'Now that I do know,' Griff continued, 'I shall of course talk to my brother. Even if his plans make it impossible for you to continue to occupy your present building, I see no reason why we shouldn't offer you alternative accommodation, perhaps within Griffiths Brothers' store.'

Jodi shook her head stubbornly. 'I don't want to be a part of Griffithses'. I want to run my boutique independently.'

He shrugged. 'That independent spirit of yours again. It stood between us for a long time—too long. Well, it's not going to stand between us again. We'll work something out, Jodi, I promise. But,' his eyes darkened and he moved towards her again, 'this, as you once said, isn't the time or the place. I don't know about you, but I have more important things on my mind——'

'More important!' She tried to sound indignant again, but failed. The boutique *was* important to her, but—as he took her in his arms again, she finally admitted it—not so important as Griff.

'Yes, more important. I want to hear you say you believe me. I want to hear you say you love me, that you'll marry me.' He studied her gravely.

She nodded. 'I believe you. And I promise I'll never doubt you again.'

'You'd better not,' he growled. 'And what about the rest?'

She felt the colour invading her cheeks. 'I love you,' she said shyly, 'and . . . and yes, I . . . I'd like to marry you. And . . . and there's something else I have to tell you.' She whispered her secret against his ear.

With an exultant little sound he gathered her close, his lips on hers, and for a long while there was silence.

Again it was Griff who broke away first. 'If I followed all that my instincts are telling me,' he said huskily, 'I'd be carrying you upstairs and making passionate love to you. But,' wryly, 'I know you have reservations about behaving that way under the parental roof—and this is your mother's house—and,' he looked at his watch, 'we have about three minutes left before she comes back.'

Jodi reached up and touched his face lovingly. 'You won't have to wait very long,' she promised him. 'I'm coming back with you—tonight.'

'You most certainly are,' he agreed. 'I'm not letting you out of my sight again until we're safely married. Why that wry little smile?' he demanded suspiciously.

'I was just thinking how pleased Sally will be—and how smug. Her dearest wish for me was a man for Christmas.'

Griff was amused. 'Is that what I am?'

Jodi stood on tiptoe and pressed her lips to his. 'Not just that,' she murmured. 'You're my man for all seasons.'

Share the adventure—and the romance—of

HARLEQUIN 〈◆〉 PRESENTS®

A Year
DOWN UNDER

If you missed any titles in this miniseries,
here's your chance to order them:

Harlequin Presents®—A Year Down Under

#11519	HEART OF THE OUTBACK by Emma Darcy	$2.89	❑
#11527	NO GENTLE SEDUCTION by Helen Bianchin	$2.89	❑
#11537	THE GOLDEN MASK by Robyn Donald	$2.89	❑
#11546	A DANGEROUS LOVER by Lindsay Armstrong	$2.89	❑
#11554	SECRET ADMIRER by Susan Napier	$2.89	❑
#11562	OUTBACK MAN by Miranda Lee	$2.99	❑
#11570	NO RISKS, NO PRIZES by Emma Darcy	$2.99	❑
#11577	THE STONE PRINCESS by Robyn Donald	$2.99	❑
#11586	AND THEN CAME MORNING by Daphne Clair	$2.99	❑
#11595	WINTER OF DREAMS by Susan Napier	$2.99	❑
#11601	RELUCTANT CAPTIVE by Helen Bianchin	$2.99	❑
#11611	SUCH DARK MAGIC by Robyn Donald	$2.99	❑

(limited quantities available on certain titles)

TOTAL AMOUNT	$
POSTAGE & HANDLING	$
($1.00 for one book, 50¢ for each additional)	
APPLICABLE TAXES*	$ _____
TOTAL PAYABLE	$ _____
(check or money order—please do not send cash)	

To order, complete this form and send it, along with a check or money order for the
total above, payable to Harlequin Books, to: *In the U.S.*: 3010 Walden Avenue,
P.O. Box 9047, Buffalo, NY 14269-9047; *In Canada*: P.O. Box 613, Fort Erie, Ontario,
L2A 5X3.

Name: _____

Address: _____ City: _____

State/Prov.: _____ Zip/Postal Code: _____

*New York residents remit applicable sales taxes.
 Canadian residents remit applicable GST and provincial taxes.

YDUF

OFFICIAL RULES • MILLION DOLLAR SWEEPSTAKES
NO PURCHASE OR OBLIGATION NECESSARY TO ENTER

To enter, follow the directions published. **ALTERNATE MEANS OF ENTRY:** Hand print your name and address on a 3"x5" card and mail to either: Harlequin "Match 3," 3010 Walden Ave., P.O. Box 1867, Buffalo, NY 14269-1867, or Harlequin "Match 3," P.O. Box 609, Fort Erie, Ontario L2A 5X3, and we will assign your Sweepstakes numbers. (Limit: one entry per envelope.) For eligibility, entries must be received no later than March 31, 1994. No responsibility is assumed for lost, late or misdirected entries.

Upon receipt of entry, Sweepstakes numbers will be assigned. To determine winners, Sweepstakes numbers will be compared against a list of randomly preselected prizewinning numbers. In the event all prizes are not claimed via the return of prizewinning numbers, random drawings will be held from among all other entries received to award unclaimed prizes.

Prizewinners will be determined no later than May 30, 1994. Selection of winning numbers and random drawings are under the supervision of D.L. Blair, Inc., an independent judging organization, whose decisions are final. One prize to a family or organization. No substitution will be made for any prize, except as offered. Taxes and duties on all prizes are the sole responsibility of winners. Winners will be notified by mail. Chances of winning are determined by the number of entries distributed and received.

Sweepstakes open to persons 18 years of age or older, except employees and immediate family members of Torstar Corporation, D.L. Blair, Inc., their affiliates, subsidiaries and all other agencies, entities and persons connected with the use, marketing or conduct of this Sweepstakes. All applicable laws and regulations apply. Sweepstakes offer void wherever prohibited by law. Any litigation within the province of Quebec respecting the conduct and awarding of a prize in this Sweepstakes must be submitted to the Régies des Loteries et Courses du Quebec. In order to win a prize, residents of Canada will be required to correctly answer a time-limited arithmetical skill-testing question. Values of all prizes are in U.S. currency.

Winners of major prizes will be obligated to sign and return an affidavit of eligibility and release of liability within 30 days of notification. In the event of non-compliance within this time period, prize may be awarded to an alternate winner. Any prize or prize notification returned as undeliverable will result in the awarding of that prize to an alternate winner. By acceptance of their prize, winners consent to use of their names, photographs or other likenesses for purposes of advertising, trade and promotion on behalf of Torstar Corporation without further compensation, unless prohibited by law.

This Sweepstakes is presented by Torstar Corporation, its subsidiaries and affiliates in conjunction with book, merchandise and/or product offerings. Prizes are as follows: Grand Prize–$1,000,000 (payable at $33,333.33 a year for 30 years). First through Sixth Prizes may be presented in different creative executions, each with the following approximate values: First Prize–$35,000; Second Prize–$10,000; 2 Third Prizes–$5,000 each; 5 Fourth Prizes–$1,000 each; 10 Fifth Prizes–$250 each; 1,000 Sixth Prizes–$100 each. Prizewinners will have the opportunity of selecting any prize offered for that level. A travel-prize option, if offered and selected by winner, must be completed within 12 months of selection and is subject to hotel and flight accommodations availability. Torstar Corporation may present this Sweepstakes utilizing names other than Million Dollar Sweepstakes. For a current list of all prize options offered within prize levels and all names the Sweepstakes may utilize, send a self-addressed, stamped envelope (WA residents need not affix return postage) to: Million Dollar Sweepstakes Prize Options/Names, P.O. Box 4710, Blair, NE 68009.

The Extra Bonus Prize will be awarded in a random drawing to be conducted no later than May 30, 1994 from among all entries received. To qualify, entries must be received by March 31, 1994 and comply with published directions. No purchase necessary. For complete rules, send a self-addressed, stamped envelope (WA residents need not affix return postage) to: Extra Bonus Prize Rules, P.O. Box 4600, Blair, NE 68009.

For a list of prizewinners (available after July 31, 1994) send a separate, stamped, self-addressed envelope to: Million Dollar Sweepstakes Winners, P.O. Box 4728, Blair, NE 68009.   SWP-H12/93

HARLEQUIN®

PRESENTS® *plus*

Meet Lily Norfolk. Not even her husband's tragic death can convince her to tell his brother, Dane Norfolk, the truth behind their marriage. It's better that he believe she married Daniel for his money and that she had an affair with Daniel's best friend. It's better that Dane keep his distance!

And then there's Elizabeth. She's a respectable young woman, but she also has a secret mission and a secret repressed sensual side. Jake Hawkwood's never liked secrets—he's determined to uncover everything Elizabeth's been hiding....

Lily and Elizabeth are just two of the passionate women you'll discover each month in Harlequin Presents Plus. And if you think they're passionate, wait until you meet Dane and Jake!

Watch for
HOUSE OF GLASS by Michelle Reid
Harlequin Presents Plus #1615
and

THE HAWK AND THE LAMB by Susan Napier
Harlequin Presents Plus #1616

Harlequin Presents Plus
The best has just gotten better!

Available in January wherever Harlequin Books are sold.